DAWN KNOX

BLETCHLEY
SECRETS

Complete and Unabridged

LINFORD
Leicester

First published in Great Britain in 2020

First Linford Edition
published 2021

*A catalogue record for this book is available
from the British Library.*

ISBN 978–1–4448–4722–2

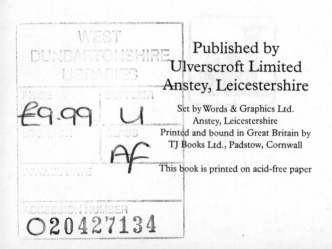

Published by
Ulverscroft Limited
Anstey, Leicestershire

Set by Words & Graphics Ltd.
Anstey, Leicestershire
Printed and bound in Great Britain by
TJ Books Ltd., Padstow, Cornwall

This book is printed on acid-free paper

BLETCHLEY SECRETS

1940: A cold upbringing with parents who unfairly blame her for a family tragedy has robbed Jess of all self-worth and confidence. Escaping to join the WAAF, she's stationed at RAF Holsmere, until a seemingly unimportant competition leads to her recruitment into the secret world of code-breaking at Bletchley Park. Love, however, eludes her: the men she chooses are totally unsuitable — until she meets Daniel. But there is so much which separates them. Can they ever find happiness together?

To my mum, I love you forever
and always

Author's Note

Most of the people who worked at Bletchley Park were women. It's said they shortened the war by up to two years, saving countless lives.

The author would like to acknowledge the following books in writing *Bletchley Secrets*:

The Secret Life of Bletchley Park, Sinclair McKay, Aurum Press Ltd

The Debs of Bletchley Park, Michael Smith, Aurum Press Ltd

The Bletchley Girls, Tessa Dunlop, Hodder & Stoughton

1

Liverpool Street Station, London 1940

Jess wouldn't allow herself to cry. She'd spent nineteen years suppressing her tears and keeping her emotions in check, and she could surely do so now.

Nevertheless, it was one of the hardest things she'd ever done — to say good-bye to Genevieve. Not that they'd been very close. Mostly, they'd been on different shifts at RAF Holsmere — but their time together had now ended and Jess was overcome by a sense of loss.

There were tears in Genevieve's eyes, Jess noted. But then she was half-French and prone to emotional responses.

'Take care and I wish you all the best,' Genevieve said, stepping forward and hugging Jess. Then, holding her at arms' length, she looked at her as if committing her face to memory.

'You too,' Jess said brightly, bending to

1

pick up her kitbag and slipping a finger behind her spectacles to wipe her eyes.

'Be safe, Genevieve,' she said as she turned and walked away, to be swallowed up by the milling crowds on the station concourse.

Jess didn't look back. There was no point.

Genevieve was about to start a new life and so was she. Neither of them had mentioned keeping in touch because she suspected Genevieve was going to be involved in something clandestine and possibly dangerous. The fact that she was bilingual with no trace of an accent and was adventurous to the point of recklessness suggested she'd been selected to do something more exciting than the work both girls had done at RAF Holsmere. Genevieve had been vague about her new posting, and Jess was certain it wasn't going to be the sort of job where she had plenty of time to write detailed letters.

And even if Jess was wrong, where would she tell Genevieve to write?

A few weeks before, Jess had attended

an unusual meeting in London after winning a crossword competition. She'd been instructed to tell no one about the meeting, nor about the possibility of her being engaged as a clerk at a place called Bletchley Park. However, other than being asked to return to Praed Street in London with a packed suitcase, she knew nothing else, not even an address to give to anyone who might write. Except, of course, her father's vicarage — in the hope her mother would remember to forward any letters.

The thought of her parents lowered her mood even more. She was on her way home before she was due back in London in two days' time.

Jess sighed and checked her watch. After leaving Genevieve, her pace had slowed as if her feet recognised her reluctance to go to Sevenoaks. Still, if she didn't want to miss the train and risk spending the night in the station, she knew she'd best hurry. She had to go home, however much she was dreading it.

'Oh, Jessica! There you are! I was beginning to get worried about you,' Mrs Langley said, although Jess suspected this was said more to let her know she was late than from any anxiety.

'Sorry, Mama. The train was late,' she lied.

'I'm afraid your lunch'll be dried up. I put it in the oven to keep warm. Mrs Carling handed in her notice a few weeks ago and I've not been able to find a replacement, so I'd appreciate all the help you can give me while you're home.'

Jess was amazed the cook had stayed so long.

'I'll be leaving the day after tomorrow, Mama.'

Mrs Langley sniffed.

'Well, so long as you're here for tomorrow . . . Papa would be most upset if you weren't.'

'I said I'd be here.' Jess bit back her irritation.

'Yes,' her mother said in her *I should*

4

think so too voice.

'I got these in the village.' Jess held out a bunch of flowers.

'Well, don't just wave them at me. They need water or they'll not last an hour.'

Jess sighed. The flowers were drooping but they were the last bunch in the shop. She knew better than to arrive with nothing for the memorial.

'Where's Papa?' she asked.

'In the study,' Mrs Langley said.

Jess's heart sank. 'Shall I go and say hello?'

'No! He doesn't want to be disturbed. He's preparing for tomorrow. He asked me to take his dinner to him — when it's ready. Now you're here, you can give me a hand.'

Jess breathed a sigh of relief. With any luck she could avoid her father until tomorrow, though the service would be a trial. But after it was over, she'd go and see Gibby. That was something to look forward to.

Dinner had been a gloomy affair, with periods of silence interspersed with Mrs Langley's complaints about the cook handing in her notice. Jess feigned tiredness and once she'd helped her mother clear away, she escaped to her bedroom.

She pulled the blackout curtains, lit a candle and sat on her bed. The room was familiar, yet unwelcoming with its ancient beams, creaking floor and musty smell. The vicarage dated back to the early eighteenth century and it was only because kind parishioners carried out frequently-needed repairs that the house was still habitable. Certainly, Rev Langley had no idea how to mend roofs or stop draughts. Worse, he'd resisted installing modern comforts such as electricity.

Mice scampered about in the attic above her bedroom. The sound of their skittering feet didn't upset Jess. She'd been used to them as a child and anyway, at Holsmere, she'd been billeted in a farmhouse which had its fair share of vermin.

She thought of Genevieve sharing time with her family — something she'd been looking forward to — and Jess envied her that.

And what about Kitty and Ellie, the two WAAFs with whom she and Genevieve had shared a billet? Ellie would probably be working an extra shift and Kitty would be out on a date. A while ago, Jess had found Ellie's intensity annoying and as for Kitty ... well, Jess had been scandalised at her loose morals. She hadn't expected to miss them.

Despite their initial coolness towards her, recently they'd shown more interest in Jess than her own mother had done — who, since she'd been home, had asked nothing about her life at the airbase. Neither had she asked where Jess would be working when she left the vicarage.

Before she'd joined the Air Force, as a WAAF, she'd assumed her mother's lack of interest in her life was because Jess hadn't done anything of consequence.

But now Mrs Langley had no idea of the things Jess had seen or done and obviously didn't want to know.

A strange thought struck her. Perhaps it wasn't so much that Jess was dull and her life uneventful and more that her mother was so engrossed in herself and life in the vicarage, she didn't consider her daughter might have anything worth telling.

The candle flickered, doing its best to light the small room where her childhood possessions were arranged. Further along the corridor was her brother's bedroom. William was five years her senior and as soon as he'd been able, he'd joined the Army. He hadn't returned since. She knew his bedroom was draped in dust cloths. After so long, no one expected him to return.

Next door was the large, airy room Jess had once shared with her elder sister, Clara. It was spotlessly clean with everything laid out neatly where Clara had left it. The only item missing was Jess' bed, which had been moved to the small room with the sloping ceiling in which she now sat. It was as if she'd been banished.

Of course, no one had suggested such a thing. That was the uncomfortable thing about life in the vicarage, no one said much at all — communication was subtle. It was to be found in her parents' silences, the merest glimmer of an expression, the barely audible sniffs or snorts. Over the years, Jess had tuned in to all those cues and could interpret their meaning.

She was gripped with an urge to see Clara's room. Had it finally been draped in dust cloths? Or was it still the pristine place she remembered?

Taking the candle, she opened the door slowly. Walking to the left side of the hall, she stepped over the creaking floorboards and at Clara's room, winced as she lifted the latch. She expected it to grate but it had obviously been oiled recently and rose silently.

Jess slipped inside, holding the candle aloft. Everything was just as she remembered.

She closed her eyes and imagined Clara sitting on the window seat, her blonde hair flopping forward as she leaned over a book.

With a start, Jess realised someone was climbing the stairs at the far end of the hall. There was no way she'd be able to get back to her bedroom without being seen, so she stood motionless, hoping her mother or father would go to their bedroom without walking along the hall. The creaking of the floorboards told her otherwise and from the lightness of the step, it was obviously her mother. Jess waited, motionless.

'What are you doing here?' Mrs Langley's voice was cold.

'Looking at my sister's room,' Jess said, surprised at her boldness. Before she'd left to join the WAAF, she'd simply have apologised if her mother had found her in Clara's room, having stolen in there like a thief — although she wouldn't have known why she was sorry, nor what she was apologising for.

'Well, now you've looked, go back

to your room. I don't know what you were thinking, bringing a candle in here. There's no blackout blind.'

Mrs Langley held the door open and regarded her daughter with cold eyes.

Jess walked past her, back to her room. She'd spoken with spirit, telling her mother she was looking at Clara's room — a place she had every right to be. Nevertheless, guilt bore down on her.

Why? Jess wondered. *How does Mama always make me feel like I'm in the wrong?*

The first time she'd returned home on leave from Holsmere, she realised how inadequate she'd felt before she'd gone away and how the confidence she'd gained working with the other WAAFs had begun to replace those feelings. But her self-belief was rapidly eroded by her mother.

It wasn't as if her mother ever said anything to undermine Jess's confidence. There was always silence, a tightening of the lips, an avoidance of eye contact, but

11

no words of condemnation which Jess might contradict or fight.

Fight. That was an interesting word, and one that only seemed to have entered her head since she'd joined the war effort. There was never any fighting in St Margaret's Vicarage. No one lost their temper. Her parents acted with the utmost propriety and therefore, she felt — as she'd always felt — that her feelings of guilt must be because she was indeed, at fault.

It's like fighting shadows, Jess thought.

She undressed, laying her clothes carefully on the chair, and climbed into bed. She'd always tried to please her mother by being tidy, helpful and quiet. But it hadn't been enough. At RAF Holsmere, she'd behaved in a similar way and had been surprised at how Ellie, Kitty and Genevieve had seen her good behaviour as obsessive. Only perceptive Genevieve, with whom she'd shared a room, had recognised her need to please people.

'Don't worry about what others think, Jess!' she'd said. 'If you don't like

yourself, you'll never please anyone —
including yourself!'

A wave of homesickness engulfed her
as she thought of her billet at Holsmere
and the three girls. She might call the
vicarage 'home' but it didn't offer sanc-
tuary. She couldn't wait for the day after
tomorrow, to be off once again.

I won't come back! she thought,
although she knew she would, because
next year around this time there'd be
another memorial service. She'd have to
return for that, or . . .

Or what? What could her parents do
if she didn't return? After all, William
never came home.

She didn't even know where he was at
the moment — his last letter to her having arrived weeks before. If she didn't
come home, her parents wouldn't be
able to do anything at all.

But what about Clara? Would she
care?

Clara with the golden hair, who had
never been the target of her parents'
silence, lip-pursing or condemnatory

sniffs. Would she mind if Jess didn't come next year?

Of course she wouldn't. Clara would understand.

* * *

Jess woke early after a disturbed sleep. She'd been dreading the memorial service — although she was looking forward to seeing Gibby, whom she'd visit on her way home.

John Gibbs, whose family had lived in the village for generations, had left and returned with a Swiss bride years before Jess was born. Apparently, it had caused quite a stir but John and Anna had lived happily for many years. By the time John died, Anna could speak English perfectly, although with a slight accent and it didn't seem to bother her that although she'd been part of the community for years, she was still seen as a foreigner.

After her husband died, she'd asked Rev Langley if he knew of anyone who wanted a cook or housekeeper and he'd suggested she work for his wife. Mrs Gibbs had been there to look after the three Langley children. During the first years of her life, Jess thought Mrs Gibbs was her mother and had been disappointed and bewildered when she'd become old enough to find out otherwise.

The day Clara died, Gibby, as Jess had come to call her, had taken time off to visit her sister-in-law, and Jess had often wondered whether things would have been different if she'd been there.

Jess had been bored. William was staying overnight with a friend and Clara was drawing in her bedroom, but Jess had pestered her until she'd agreed to play hide and seek in the garden. It had been a beautiful autumn afternoon and the leaves were beginning to fall, although the large oak in the meadow still had enough foliage to hide a small eight-year-old among its branches.

Jess had peeped out at the garden and watched Clara half-heartedly searching behind bushes and peering into the interior of the shed through the dirty window.

She'd watched her sister until she'd got as far as the bottom of the garden and disappeared from sight. Jess began to get cramp in her foot and wondered when Clara would come back and find her. The earlier satisfaction at having found a successful hiding place faded, to be replaced by annoyance at her sister for taking so long to find her.

She'd begun to suspect Clara had crept back to her bedroom and resumed her drawing, or perhaps had silently approached the tree and would jump out at her when she climbed down. Jess listened carefully for anything which would give her a clue and then realised that some way off, she could hear screams and splashing.

Could Clara have gone down by the river? Surely not! The children had been forbidden to go there alone. She crawled backwards along the branch to the trunk but in her haste, slipped and fell, hitting a lower branch before landing awkwardly on her side. Getting to her feet, she hobbled towards the fence at the bottom of the garden, screaming Clara's name.

Her father had heard her shouts and run out, pushing her to one side and climbing the fence.

She didn't remember much after that, other than explaining to a constable what she'd seen, then staying at Gibby's cottage.

By the time she'd returned home, Clara had been buried in St Margaret's churchyard and Jess's bed had been moved into the small room where she was now lying.

From then on, Jess spent as much time as she was allowed with Gibby, either in the vicarage or in her cottage, helping with chores. While they worked, Gibby told Jess about her childhood in Switzerland, teaching her words in French, German and Italian and offering her the attention she didn't receive at home.

'Your parents are grieving, Jess,' Gibby said on many occasions. 'They need time to come to terms with the loss of their daughter. When you're older, you'll understand.'

But as the years passed, she no longer made excuses for her employers' lack of interest in their remaining daughter. Even Jess's brother, William, who being several years older had always ignored her, seemed to notice his parents' inattention towards his sister and spent time with her, teaching her to play chess and card games — until one day, he'd argued with his father and left home to join the Army. He'd never returned, although he wrote to Jess regularly.

After war broke out, Jess decided to become a WAAF. The idea of flying away and escaping appealed to her, even though she knew WAAFs didn't actually fly aircraft. Gibby encouraged her, which was just as well; without her reassurance, Jess would have lacked the confidence to leave home. St Margaret's Vicarage might be a loveless place but at least it was familiar.

As Jess had anticipated, her announcement that she'd joined up was met with mild interest. Although once Mrs Langley realised that when Jess left, Mrs Gibbs intended to hand in her notice, she was displeased at being left without a house-keeper and made her opinions very clear.

Once Mrs Langley was no longer her employer, Mrs Gibbs made her own opinions very clear.

'I've never seen such cold-hearted parents! Your treatment of Jess is nothing less than scandalous.'

'How dare you!' Mrs Langley had shouted. 'My daughter's no concern of yours. She's lacked nothing under my roof — '

'Nothing, except love!'

'What do you know? You're not a mother!'

'I know enough to see that a child needs kindness and attention. Jess has been your scapegoat for too long.'

'Scapegoat? How dare you! You don't know what you're talking about!'

'You've taken your guilt out on Je — '

'Out of my house! Get out! And don't ever come back! All those people who told me I'd regret employing a foreigner were right! You've no idea how we behave in England — '

Jess had cried as she'd watched Gibby walk down the path of the vicarage into the lane for the last time. If she'd had any qualms about leaving the place which hadn't been a true home since Clara had died, they faded as Gibby disappeared around the bend in the lane. She'd longed for the day when she'd leave to train as a WAAF.

* * *

At breakfast Rev Langley greeted Jess in a perfunctory way, enquiring if she was well and about her journey. As if she were a guest — not his only surviving daughter returning from an RAF station which had been targeted during the Battle of Britain.

'We'll start at ten o'clock,' he said in the voice he used to announce notices in church. 'There will be a brief service, then prayers at the gr . . . '

Jess could see his Adam's apple bobbing up and down as he swallowed, trying to keep control of his emotions.

He couldn't continue but she knew he meant at Clara's graveside.

Mrs Langley nodded to show she understood.

The rest of the breakfast was eaten in silence.

The sooner it begins, the sooner it'll be over. Jess consoled herself with the thought of seeing Gibby again. She hadn't received a letter from her for several weeks — Gibby's arthritis made it hard for her to write. How lovely it would be to see her.

* * *

Everything in the church was as Jess remembered — the grey stone walls and pillars, and its upright, uncomfortable pews. The stained glass normally sparkled in the sunlight but cloudy skies threatened rain and the colourful images in the windows were muted and dull. Even the flowers were drooping. Several petals had fallen prematurely and now lay on the flagstones.

How many times had Jess sat in this same pew, listening to her father speak about the wages of sin and the path to destruction? But today, there was no fire in him. Her mother sat next to her, not holding her hand nor even linking arms. Straight-backed and rigid, she suffered in her own way, not seeking consolation from Jess, nor giving any.

Finally, Rev Langley finished. Closing his Bible, he paused at the lectern for a few seconds of private prayer and then marched down the aisle without looking at his wife or daughter.

Jess and her mother followed him outside and after prayers at Clara's graveside, they laid flowers on the neatly-kept grave and stood waiting for Rev Langley to dismiss them.

It was over. Jess said a silent farewell to her sister and placing a kiss on the tips of her fingers, she touched the headstone.

Rev and Mrs Langley turned to go.

'Mama, I'll be back to help you with lunch but I'd like to say hello to Mrs Gibbs, if that's all right.'

'Mrs Gibbs?' Mrs Langley frowned.

'Yes.' Surely her mother hadn't forgotten the woman who'd worked in her house for years.

'But Mrs Gibbs died two weeks ago,' Mrs Langley said.

If Mrs Langley had slapped her, Jess couldn't have been more shocked.

'D . . . died? B . . . but . . . how can that be?'

'I heard it was a heart problem. She was ill for a few days before she died.'

'And you didn't think to tell me?'

Jess couldn't believe her mother hadn't bothered to let her know — nor that she was speaking in such a detached way. It was as if she were discussing the weather!

'I'm sure I did. And anyway, I don't believe you've written to me for a few weeks.' Jess remained silent. Frozen. So many thoughts tumbled through her brain. And memories — happy memories of the woman who'd loved her and been her surrogate mother.

'She's buried over there with her husband,' Mrs Langley said, pointing across the graveyard. As her mother followed her father home, Jess walked slowly to the Gibbs' grave, allowing the tears to run unchecked down her cheeks.

She stayed a while by the freshly-dug grave. It didn't seem possible that she'd never see gentle Gibby again. During the previous few months, she'd been aware of so many senseless deaths, so many young pilots barely out of training, whose aircraft hadn't come home. But this! Perhaps it was the shocking way her mother had delivered the news, but Jess was finding it hard to believe.

She arrived back at the vicarage in time to help her mother prepare lunch. After her father said Grace, Jess expected there to be silence during the meal but Rev Langley wanted to talk.

'Clara would have been at university now.'

'Yes,' agreed Mrs Langley. 'She was so gifted at mathematics. Just like you, dear,' she added, patting her husband's hand.

'I obviously passed it on to her,' he said, shaking his head sadly. 'She'd have loved university. And then she'd have found an excellent job in an office.'

Jess said nothing. Clara had been clever and particularly gifted at mathematics, it was true, but she'd been ten when she died — far too early to predict whether she'd get to university or even if she'd want to go. She'd been a pretty child, and showed promise of growing into a beautiful woman. Perhaps by now, she'd have met someone and had a family. But there was no point voicing her thoughts. Clara's future had been discussed in great detail at other Langley meals, and the impossibility of it existing didn't stop her parents from inventing a story and then clinging to it as if it were reality.

Jess felt torn. She'd loved her sister and cherished her memory, but she knew her parents' idealised love for their dead child filled their hearts and eclipsed any affection they may have saved for her. Clara was perfect. Jess would always be flawed. Clara was gifted and beautiful. Jess knew she was neither.

Gibby had tried to convince her otherwise, pointing out that she, too, was excellent at mathematics and problem-solving. And who was to say which sister was more intelligent? Jess was two years younger than Clara. Perhaps Jess would have exceeded her sister's abilities one day. No one would ever know.

And Jess had a different beauty. She had a doll-like, delicate appearance with dark curls framing an oval face and skin as smooth as porcelain. Her glasses had bothered her but Gibby said Jess was so lovely, people wouldn't even notice she was wearing them. Jess knew she was just saying that to cheer her up, but it was touching that she bothered to try to bolster Jess's confidence.

'And how do you see your future unfolding, Jess?' Rev Langley asked.

Jess had been so lost in her own thoughts, she'd missed the question.

'Sorry, Papa?'

Her father repeated his question. She could see in his eyes, it was more of a test than an idle contemplation of his daughter's life.

'Well . . . I . . . I don't know,' she stuttered, not having expected to be asked anything. 'I suppose I shall have to wait for the war to be over.'

'I hear many girls in the services are taking the opportunity to behave in a loose and immoral manner,' he said in a way which suggested he was challenging Jess to defend herself.

'Well, I don't know any of them,' Jess said firmly. It wasn't true, of course — Kitty had been the most obvious example of someone who'd behaved in a loose and immoral manner and she was by no means the only one. 'The WAAFs are doing a wonderful job of assisting the RAF pilots in defending Great Britain. We work long hours, often all through the night. There's no time for loose and immoral behaviour,' she added.

'Yes, indeed. Well, see that you remember all you learned about leading a good, upright life.'

Jess was amazed at her father's agreement. She'd expected a lecture on the importance of maintaining morals and standards.

'Clara was always such a good child . . .' Mrs Langley said and the conversation between the vicar and his wife turned once more to all Clara had achieved and would undoubtedly have gone on to accomplish, had she not been taken from them at such a young age.

When the meal was finally concluded, Jess once again felt the great weight of guilt bearing down on her. There had been no blame apportioned — well, none that had been spoken. But glances, sighs and shakes of the head conveyed to Jess that a great deal of the culpability was hers.

Once the meal was over, Jess helped her mother clear the table and wash up. As she was about to go to bed, Mrs Langley said, 'Oh, Jess, I nearly forgot. There's a box for you on the mantel-piece. Mrs Gibbs left it for you.'

'You nearly forgot?' Jess asked incredulously.

'Well,' her mother said, bristling, 'this

time of year is always difficult.' She glanced pointedly at the framed photograph of Clara on the sideboard.

★ ★ ★

Once upstairs, Jess sat with the long parcel on her lap, reluctant to open the paper because by doing so, it would simply be another reminder that the woman she'd loved really had gone.

It was so typical of her mother to turn the subject back to Clara when Jess had expressed dismay at her forgetting to tell her about the parcel. Although, to be fair, the conversation hadn't been turned at all. There had been no words. Simply a glance at Clara's photograph.

Was she being too sensitive? Was she reading more into her parents' behaviour and mannerisms than was actually there? She didn't know, and there was no one to ask. No one to hold her and comfort her, making sense of it all.

Jess held the parcel against her cheek and closed her eyes. The delicate scent of beeswax and lavender lingered on the paper, and Jess breathed in, wanting to surround herself with the smell. But the more she tried to savour it, the fainter it became until it was overwhelmed by the dust and damp of her bedroom.

Jess peeled back the paper to reveal a jewellery box. She guessed what was inside. How many times had she admired the string of pearls Gibby always wore? They had been a gift from John on her wedding day and Gibby had always said they would be Jess's one day.

Opening the catch, Jess raised the lid, once again detecting the scent of beeswax and lavender. She took the necklace out and held it up, admiring it, then allowed its satin-smoothness to run through her fingers. Tucked inside the lid was a letter.

Dear Jess,

By the time you receive this, I will have joined my beloved John. Please don't be sad. I had a good life filled with love. It would have been wonderful to have seen Switzerland again before I died but it was not to be. Perhaps one day when the world is at peace, you will go there for me?

My heart problem came on suddenly and there is nothing the doctors can do, so I know I only have a short time. I have asked for the necklace you loved to be delivered to St Margaret's Vicarage and I hope you will find it next time you are home.

I know you are about to start a new post and I wish you all luck. Remember, Jess, you are clever, kind, loving and beautiful. Hopefully the people who fill your life will remind you of that often.

I will be watching over you, my darling girl.

Trudi Gibbs.

Jess blew out the candle and sat in the dark.

Hopefully the people who fill your life will remind you of that often. So far, Gibby had been the only person who'd done that.

Had Jess remained at Holsmere longer

31

and allowed herself to open up to the other girls, she wondered if they might also have made her feel valuable. But one thing was certain — her parents' lives were so full of Clara, there was no room for her. She wondered if they'd treated William in the same offhand way. She'd been too young to notice her brother's relationship with their parents but if it had been good, surely he'd have returned to see them.

It occurred to her that there was no reason for her to ever return, now Gibby had gone. There would be a memorial service next year for Clara, but Jess could honour her sister and remember her wherever she was — she didn't need to come back to the vicarage. From now on, home would be wherever she decided it would be.

Jess re-lit the candle and looked through the drawers and cupboards for anything she wanted to take when she left the following day. There was very little. A book Clara used to read to her and a few of Clara's drawings. Jess packed them ready to leave early next morning.

She had an urge to see Clara's room one last time. Taking the candle, she opened the door and walked along the hall, heedless of the creaks. First, she went into William's room. Pulling back a dust sheet, she opened his desk drawer and found the box of chess pieces they'd once played with. She selected the white queen and the black king and put them in her pocket. Replacing the cloth, she went into Clara's room.

Removing a photograph of the three Langley children from a frame on the table, Jess made her way back, not creeping as she had previously.

Why should I feel guilty about going to my brother's and sister's bedrooms to say goodbye?

If either of her parents heard her, they didn't come upstairs to investigate. Jess went back in her bedroom and packed the book, drawings, chess pieces and photograph. There was nothing else she wanted from this house.

Jess rose early next morning and made a sandwich for lunch while she hastily ate some breakfast. As she was finishing her tea, she noticed marks on the door frame.

Crouching down, she inspected them. The Langley children's heights, marked with their ages. The last measurements finished when Clara was ten and William, thirteen. Jess's height appeared twice — at age four and six.

Why hadn't her height been recorded each year along with her brother's and sister's? It was as if she'd been an afterthought. The forgotten one. These marks appeared to be not so much records of how fast the children had grown, but more a gauge of their parents' affections.

The lump in Jess's throat prevented her from swallowing the rest of the tea. She tipped it into the sink, then washed up and wiped down the table as her mother liked, and left the vicarage.

She closed the door and walked down the path to the lane. The church was a silhouette against the dawn sky. It seemed to observe her disapprovingly as she said goodbye to Clara and Gibby at their graves. Then she turned and walked briskly to the railway station.

2

After catching the first train from Seven-oaks, Jess arrived at Paddington Station early. She picked her way carefully along the platform, which was still covered in sleeping people who'd been sheltering overnight from air raids.

Many others, clutching children, bedding and bags, accompanied her as she climbed to street level. They poured out into Praed Street, blinking in the daylight after the night spent underground. After checking their family groups were together, they trudged home wearily. How many would find a pile of rubble where they'd once lived? Already those who wished to buy a platform ticket and ensure a place in the station that night, had started to queue by the entrance. Jess hurried past them. She found the anonymous-looking building she'd visited a few weeks before and checked her watch. In her haste to avoid her parents, she'd arrived five hours early — but she knew there was a small café not far away where she could buy a cup of tea and wait a few hours. Perhaps she'd go for a walk after that.

As she turned into the side street, she smelled dust, smoke and charred timber — the aftermath of the previous night's bombing raid. At the far end of the road, people were staring dejectedly at a huge pile of bricks and broken wood which Jess assumed was all that remained of their home. They were carrying bedding, so had returned from a night in the air raid shelter — or even the station she'd just come from.

The café had been damaged in a previous raid and was boarded up. Someone had painted a notice on the wood to say the building was unsafe but the café would open as soon as possible and had added a cartoon of a terrified Hitler running away on spindly legs from a ferocious bulldog snapping at his heels. Even in the midst of such devastation, people still had a sense of humour, Jess thought. She checked her watch again but only a few minutes had passed. Time was going to drag if she didn't find something to do until one o'clock. She walked back to Praed Street and on a whim, caught a bus towards Central London.

In Trafalgar Square, Jess ate the sandwich she'd brought, then wandered around Mayfair on her way back to Praed Street. It was the first time she'd had chance to explore London and she wondered why she hadn't visited while at Holsmere. Many WAAFs would head straight for the capital as soon as they had leave. One had found a shop in Regent Street that sold undergarments made of German parachute silk. When she'd told her friends back at Holsmere, Jess had expressed surprise that anyone would want anything other than warm, comfortable underwear. She knew her mother wouldn't approve of anything other than regulation WAAF knickers. Kitty had exploded with laughter and Jess had been embarrassed at her explanation.

Now, Jess wondered what it would feel like to wear silk next to her skin. If she'd had time, she'd have looked for the shop but she was afraid she'd be late for her interview.

Why had she been so dull and unadventurous? She realised it was probably because of her father's warnings to lead a moral life. It had made her reluctant to do anything out of the ordinary.

Well, she was going to make up for lost time.

* * *

Miss Parker began the interview, asking about her background and taking notes. She seemed interested that Jess was the daughter of a vicar and had a fair grasp of French and German.

'We are looking for honest, upright girls. Now, please translate both of these into English,' she said placing two sheets of paper on the desk. Jess's heart sank. Each piece described parts of an aeroplane cockpit and engine. She did her best, guessing some words, but most of the paper she handed back to Miss Parker was blank.

Jess felt sick. She knew she'd failed the test. Would she be able to return to RAF Holsmere? She certainly wasn't going home. Miss Parker spoke to Jess in German, informing her she would be working shifts and her pay would be £120 per annum until she was twenty-one.

'Est-ce que vous me comprenez?' Miss Parker asked switching to French when Jess merely stared at her.

Jess replied in French that she did understand, it was simply that she'd assumed she'd failed.

'I would have been most surprised if you'd have been able to translate the technical texts I gave you. However, I can see you used deduction and some intelligent guesses. And for those reasons, I believe you are exactly the sort of girl we're looking for at Bletchley Park, Miss Langley. However, you must understand that if you take this job, there will be no opportunity to leave until the war is over. Do you understand?'

'Y . . . yes! Thank you.'

'And one last thing, Miss Langley,' Miss Parker said sliding a document across the desk towards her, 'This is the Official Secrets Act. Before you leave here, you need to sign it. After that, you won't be able to discuss your work with anyone. And I mean anyone. Is that fully understood?'

* * *

As Jess left the building on her way to Euston Station, she still didn't know what work she'd be doing at Bletchley Park. She'd asked several times but, on each occasion, Miss Parker had simply changed topic or replied with another question. Jess wished she'd persisted until she'd been given an answer but she'd been afraid of antagonising Miss Parker.

Once she'd signed the Official Secrets Act, she'd been given a travel warrant plus instructions on how to get to Bletchley Park and had been dismissed. It was rather disturbing. She'd been sworn to secrecy about something she knew nothing about. Well, the secrecy part at least would be easy. After all, who might she tell?

The train from Euston had been delayed and she arrived at Bletchley Station as night was drawing in. All the passengers who'd alighted walked with purpose towards the exit as if they were regulars at this station, except for Jess and another girl. Unlike Jess who was wearing her WAAF uniform, the other girl wore civilian clothes — a dark coat and hat — although like Jess, she was clutching a suitcase. 'Excuse me, you wouldn't be going to Bletchley Park by any chance, would you?'

'Yes — are you?' Jess asked.

'I am. I was given directions but I hadn't realised it'd be almost dark. I haven't brought a torch. Have you? I'm Alice Wilson, by the way.'

'Jessica Langley. Pleased to meet you.

42

Yes, I've got a torch in my kit.'

'I think this is disgraceful! They should've sent someone to meet us. Fancy expecting us to find our own way there,' Alice said.

'I don't think it's far. The lady who interviewed me said the estate was right next to the station and I'd simply need to follow the fence to the entrance.'

'Miss Parker? Oh, she interviewed me too. She didn't tell me that. She just gave me written instructions. But then, she seemed rather angry.'

'Angry?'

'Yes. I insisted she tell me what the job was about but she told me to wait and see. I nearly didn't come but my curiosity got the better of me.'

'I'm not sure what I'm going to be doing either. Miss Parker was quite vague.' Jess thought back to her interview and wondered if the girl was exaggerating her insistence on being given a job description. Surely no one would be that pushy?

In the deepening twilight, the girls

struggled up the sloping, rutted path with their suitcases. It ran along the perimeter of the park, which was surrounded by a high, chained fence topped with a roll of barbed wire.

Finally they reached the sentry box at the entrance. After checking their papers, the guard let them through with a wink and the cheery greeting of, 'Welcome to the biggest lunatic asylum in Britain.'

'What do you mean?' Alice asked.

'You'll see.'

'I don't like the sound of that,' Alice said when they were out of earshot.

'It's probably his idea of a joke,' Jess said, as the mansion came into view, dark and brooding.

She'd expected it to be similar to RAF Holsmere with everyone in uniform, bustling about with great efficiency. But once through the front door of the mansion, she was amazed to see several young men and women in civilian clothes, chatting animatedly in a group.

'Over there,' an intense-looking woman said when Jess asked where she could

44

find Commander Denniston, the head of GC&CS — the Government Code and Cypher School. She pointed to a door at the end of the corridor, without looking at Jess or Alice, still engrossed in conversation with a man who was jabbing the air with the stem of his pipe to emphasise his argument.

The door to the office was open. As Jess was about to knock, a woman seated at a desk inside called for them to enter. She rose to greet them, introducing herself as Barbara Abernethy, the personal assistant of Commander Denniston.

'The commander should be back any second,' she said, indicating they should sit on the chairs in front of his desk.

A short man in a civilian suit entered. It didn't occur to Jess he could be Commander Denniston because she expected him to be in uniform but he moved towards his desk, smiling at the girls.

'Excellent! I've been expecting you. Now I understand one of you young ladies speaks French fluently and the other has a reasonable grasp of French

45

and German.'

Alice explained her mother was French, her father was English and she'd lived in England since she was five, so was fluent in both languages.

'I understand a professor at Cambridge University recommended you?' he asked Alice.

'Professor Trevelyan is my godfather. He put my name forward.'

Jess began to wonder if they'd made a mistake recruiting her. She didn't know anyone who worked in a university, nor who would recommend her. It was just the crossword competition which seemed to have brought her to anyone's attention.

'And you are the lady who speaks passable French and German?' The commander abruptly turned his attention to Jess, making her jump.

'Y . . . yes, sir.'

'And I understand you responded to our test and passed.'

'Sir?'

'The crossword competition you completed.'

'Oh . . . I see. Yes, sir.'

'We have urgent need of people with puzzle-solving skills as well as a knowledge of languages, particularly German and French. Now, I know you've both signed the Official Secrets Act but I can't emphasise enough how imperative it is that you speak about your work to no one. Do you both understand?'

Alice and Jess nodded.

I understand it's forbidden to speak about the work, thought Jess, *I only wish I knew what that work involved.*

She caught Alice's eye and knew she was thinking the same thing but she'd obviously decided not to risk angering Commander Denniston as she had Miss Parker.

There was a tap at the door and a young woman wearing the khaki uniform of the Mechanised Transport Corps entered.

'Ah, Phyllis! Excellent, you're early,' Commander Denniston said, standing and taking his overcoat and hat from the coat stand. 'I wonder if we could detour slightly and drop these young ladies at their billet. It's . . . ' He leaned forward to check the details on his desk as he slipped his arm in his coat, 'Brick Lane. Number sixteen.'

'Of course, sir,' said Phyllis in an upper-class accent. She smiled at Jess and Alice.

Phyllis helped the girls into the back of a shooting brake outside the front door of the mansion and Commander Denniston climbed in the passenger seat next to her. She drove slowly along Brick Lane until she found number sixteen, a grimy, terraced house halfway along. She dropped the two girls off, then drove away.

'What a dreadful smell,' Alice said as she knocked on the door of the terraced house.

'Yes?' The woman who answered the door scowled at them.

'Mrs Grady?'

'Who's askin'?'

'Alice Wilson and Jessica Langley from Bletchley Park. We understand we're billeted with you,' Alice said.

48

'You're early. I wasn't expecting no one until tomorrer,' she said crossing her arms over her large bosom.

'I'm so sorry,' Jess said, worried the woman might slam the door shut.

Mrs Grady surveyed her unwanted guests.

'Well, I s'pose you'd better come in.' She stood back to let them pass.

'You've missed supper,' she said peevishly.

Jess was hungry. She hadn't eaten since she'd been in Trafalgar Square earlier that day but she didn't want to antagonise their reluctant landlady.

Alice, however, wasn't going to bed without something to eat.

'Well, I'm sure you must have a slice of bread or something for us to eat, Mrs Grady. And a cup of tea would be lovely, thank you.'

Jess held her breath waiting to be propelled towards the front door but Mrs Grady merely tutted irritably and led the way into the kitchen.

'Bread an' drippin',' she said, placing

49

two plates on the table and then returning with two mugs of weak tea.

When the girls had finished, she led
the way upstairs to a chilly bedroom.

'Bathnight's Friday,' she said, 'And
my Frank works shifts, so I don't want
no noise.'

'But suppose we're working a shift on
Friday night?' Alice asked.

'No bath,' said Mrs Grady. She turned
to go.

'Wait! Where's the other bedroom?'
Alice called.

'What other bedroom? I ain't got no
other bedroom. Yer'll 'ave to share.'

'But there's only one bed!' Alice
exclaimed.

'That's because I only got one bed.
Anyway, it's a double! Take it or leave it!'

Alice sighed.

'There must be some mistake,' said
Jess, 'but let's sort it out tomorrow.
We've got to be up early and Phyllis said
it'd take about fifteen minutes to walk to
Bletchley — that is, if we don't get lost.
And I'm so tired now.'

Neither girl slept well. The lumpy mattress sagged in the middle, and they soon discovered the house wasn't far from the railway line. Periodically, trains thundered along the track, making the house shake.

Mr Grady returned in the early hours and although he hadn't known about the arrival of the two girls, he didn't show any consideration for his wife as he slammed the front door and noisily made his way up the stairs. Minutes later, his snores reverberated throughout the house.

Breakfast was bread and dripping with weak tea and Jess hoped outspoken Alice wouldn't criticise and push Mrs Grady too far. But it seemed her roommate was too tired and worried about starting the new job to pick an argument with the landlady.

'I hope she feeds us something a bit more appetising tonight,' Alice said. Jess was grateful Mrs Grady had gone into the backyard and not overheard, although she too fervently hoped there would be a proper meal for them later.

There was a knock at the door and Mrs Grady, with a cat under one arm hurried to open it. 'Yes?' she asked indignantly. 'I wonder if you could tell me if Alice and Jessica are still here.'

'Can you keep your voice down, please! My husband's asleep. You'd better come in.'

Jess was putting her jacket on when Mrs Grady led Phyllis into the room.

'Good morning! I've got to pick up Commander Denniston early from the Park, so I thought as I was passing Brick Lane and it's your first day, I'd see if you'd like a lift into work. It was too dark to see the way last night.'

'I hope Miss Hoity-Toity's not going to make a habit of banging on my door early in the morning,' Mrs Grady said to Jess and Alice as they followed Phyllis outside. 'My husband needs his sleep,' she added, closing the door.

'What a dump,' Alice said as she looked back at the house, 'No wonder it smells so awful! Just look at that huge chimney belching out smoke.'

'That's the London Brick Company, behind the houses,' said Phyllis. 'I'm afraid you haven't got a very nice billet.'

'Oh, don't worry, I'm not going to be there for long,' said Alice.

★ ★ ★

Commander Denniston's secretary, Miss Abernethy, gave Jess and Alice a brief tour of the mansion.

'We're expanding all the time and as new huts are built, departments move into them, so what I'm showing you today probably will have changed in a few weeks. Not long ago, MI6 were on the top floor, the Naval section were crammed in the loggia and the library, the Air people were in the wooden-panelled room you passed on your way into the mansion near the Military and Diplomatic Sections. But, thankfully, they've gone to pastures new and now a lot of our administrative work is done up here,' Miss Abernethy explained as she led them upstairs.

'MI6?' Alice asked.

'Indeed.' Miss Abernethy didn't appear to find the presence of the Secret Intelligence Service in the mansion anything out of the ordinary.

'There are still lots of reminders of the previous owners, the Leon family,' Miss Abernethy continued. 'Like this office ... ' She pointed at a closed door. 'This is where you'll find Colonel Tiltman. He's a cryptanalyst and head of Military Section. His room used to be the Leon children's nursery and it's still decorated with Peter Rabbit wallpaper.'

If Jess hadn't been so worried about making a good impression on Commander Denniston's personal assistant, she'd have laughed. The head of Military Section in a room decorated with Peter Rabbit? Since she'd first acted on the letter which told her she'd won the crossword competition, life had taken on a surreal quality.

'And if you look out of this window,'

Miss Abernethy said, 'you have a good view of the lake and the grounds. Last January, the water froze over and we all went skating. And over there,' she pointed, 'you can see a new hut going up.'

'Is it some sort of shed?' Alice asked.

'No. It'll house offices just like the others you can see. That one, on the right, next to the mansion is Hut 4 and that one over there near the lake is Hut 8. They're part of the naval section.'

'You mean people work in them?' Alice's voice was incredulous, 'But they look so . . . well . . . basic. I mean, they're just wooden buildings.'

'That's exactly what they are, Miss Wilson. They are, as their names suggest, huts. Many people work in them quite satisfactorily. Without complaint.' Miss Abernethy's voice had hardened.

'Yes, yes, of course,' Alice said. 'I'm sure they're perfectly fine.'

Jess saw the corner of Miss Abernethy's lips twitch slightly as she added, 'And you, Miss Wilson, will be finding out exactly how fine because you'll be working in Hut 3, where I believe you will be involved in some sort of translation work.'

Alice scowled out of the window at the single-storey wooden buildings and Jess wondered which one she'd be working in. Her grasp of French and German wasn't perfect and after the test she'd taken with Miss Parker, she doubted she'd be able to do much translation without further study. But no one had mentioned training.

Well, ask! she told herself.

She knew she wouldn't. Had Alice not annoyed Miss Abernethy, she might have dared but she didn't want to appear as if she was complaining.

Don't be such a ninny!

But she'd spent a lifetime trying to please. And it wasn't as if being forthright had benefited Alice.

'Now, if you'd like to follow me, I'll take you to your offices,' Miss Abernethy said, heading for the stairs. 'Oh, and by the way, perhaps I ought to point out

that some of the people at Bletchley are
. . . um, shall we say . . . rather unconventional.'

'Unconventional?' Alice asked. 'In
what way?'

'In many ways,' said Miss Abernethy
firmly.

★ ★ ★

'You only have access to the place where
you work. You won't be allowed in anywhere else. Is that understood?' Miss
Abernethy said as they arrived at Hut 3.

Jess waited outside while Alice was
taken in to meet her new boss.

Miss Abernethy came out minutes
later.

'I'm not sure your friend is going to be
very happy working there,' she said, her
mouth set.

'She's not my friend,' Jess said. 'I only
met her yesterday.'

Miss Abernethy's face relaxed. 'Well,
if you want to get on, I suggest you don't
complain or criticise as much as Miss

Wilson. It's not an endearing quality. Right — now if you follow me, I'll take you to the stable yard.'

Stable yard?

'But don't worry,' Miss Abernethy continued with a smile, 'your job doesn't involve anything to do with horses. There are several buildings surrounding the stable yard — the bungalow which used to be the apple and pear store, and three cottages opposite. You'll be in one of those.'

Miss Abernethy led Jess to the back of the mansion. 'We have several top cryptanalysts working at Bletchley. Alan Turing works in this one; Dillwyn Knox — or Dilly, as everyone calls him, works there; and Thomas Kemp, who you'll be assisting, spends most of his time here.'

She raised her hand to knock on the door of the bungalow, then paused and whispered, 'They're all brilliant but . . . shall we say . . . rather eccentric. Their behaviour can be . . . erm . . . rather challenging. So,' she lowered her voice further, 'it's best not to take things personally. Your friend, Alice, certainly wouldn't have the temperament to work with our university dons in the cottages.'

Without waiting for Jess to reply, she rapped sharply on the door. 'Oh, and don't expect the usual niceties, like waiting to be invited in when you knock on a door. Just go in or you'll be on the doorstep all day.'

Jess noticed that despite her words, she hesitated slightly before entering.

As she opened the door, a screwed-up ball of paper flew across the room.

'Good morning, Tom,' Miss Abernethy said, but although the man at the desk looked up, he didn't appear to see them and waved a hand in a manner which could have been a greeting or possibly a request not to disturb him. With his elbow on the desk, he rested his forehead on his hand, hiding most of his face and his dark fringe flopping over his fingers. Jess could only see part of his face but she guessed he was a few years older than her. He wore a striped shirt beneath a sleeveless Fair Isle sweater, which appeared to be unravelling at the shoulder.

Miss Abernethy clicked her tongue disapprovingly and muttered beneath her breath, 'Pyjamas!' It took Jess a few seconds to realise she was referring to the striped shirt.

'Well, at least he remembered to put suit trousers on today,' Miss Abernethy whispered, looking down at the long legs which protruded from under the desk. She picked her way across the floor, pointedly avoiding balls of paper and the piles of files and folders.

Tom looked up, pushed his heavy-rimmed spectacles up his nose, blinked and observed his visitors with a frown.

'This is Jessica Langley,' Miss Abernethy said. 'She'll be working with you.'

Tom's gaze slid from her to Jess and back again, then running his fingers through his fringe absentmindedly, he said, 'We're breaking machines. Find a pencil, Miss . . . err. There are some rods on that desk. When you've found them, have a go at this.' He held a piece of paper out which was covered in sets of five letters.

Jess took the paper. It had a brown stain on one corner and she stared at it, not knowing what it was, much less what to do with it.

'Well, I'm sure you'll soon get the hang of it,' Miss Abernethy said, 'eventually. In the meantime, I don't think it'd go amiss if you tidied up a bit.' She stooped to pick up a crumpled piece of paper, dropped it in the waste paper basket then brushed her hands together. With a sympathetic glance at Jess, she left.

So, this was her new workplace. Jess surveyed the room. The striped wallpaper was stained brown in one corner suggesting a leaking roof, and beneath the windows it was peeling away from the wall. The blackout curtains were still half-drawn, making the room even gloomier than it might have been, and the smell of damp competed with stale pipe smoke and a rotten odour which seemed to be coming from the waste paper bin in the corner. It was surrounded by heaps of screwed-up balls of paper as if Tom had been throwing them from his desk — and mostly missing.

Tom looked up, startled as if he'd forgotten she was there, 'Found a pencil yet?'

'Err, no. I'm sorry, Mr Kemp. I'm not sure where to look.'

'It's Professor Kemp. But call me Tom. We don't stand on ceremony around here. Just clear a few things away. You'll find a pencil on your desk. Just don't touch these.' He indicated several piles of folders and papers. 'But the rest can probably go in the bin. Are you a good shot?'

'Err, do you mean with a gun?'

'Certainly not!' He screwed up another sheet of paper and threw it across the room. It hit the wall and bounced off, dropping in the bin. 'Because, if you are, we play rounders most days after lunch. You're welcome to join us . . . Ah!' he said, glancing back at the array of papers in front of him. 'I wonder if that could possibly be a 'D' . . . '

Jess moved a man's bedroom slipper and a crumb-covered plate off the collapsible chair behind the desk that Tom had indicated would be hers, then brushed the seat with her handkerchief. She picked up the paper on the floor and off her desk and crammed it in the bin, then collected all the dirty cups, saucers and plates and piled them on her desk. Suppose she accidentally threw away something Tom really wanted?

She was stacking the files she'd found on the floor with some similar ones on a shelf when a smartly-dressed man entered.

'Tom, I'm off to get some tea. Fancy a cup?' He stopped in surprise when he saw Jess standing on a box, reaching up to the shelf. 'Good lord, what's Tom got you doing? Do be careful, that box doesn't look very safe!'

Tom looked up and frowned slightly at Jess, as if wondering who she was. After glancing up at the ceiling for a second, recognition lit up his face.

'This is Miss err . . . and she's searching for a pencil. Be a good chap, give her a hand, will you? I feel like I'm making a bit of headway with this . . . '

'Welcome, Miss Err. I'm Louis Gresham.' The newcomer smiled and held out his hand to help her down off the box. 'I'm not sure you're going to find any pencils on that shelf but you've made a brave start on all the muddle in here. I came over this morning and it looked like someone had been having a snowball fight.' Jess Langley,' she said nervously. Judging by the immaculate suit and shiny shoes, this man was obviously someone senior to scruffy Tom.

'Well, Jess, how about I help you tidy the rest and then I'll show you where to empty the waste paper basket? We can get some tea then. We don't have cleaners in Bletchley Park. The fewer people who come and go the better, so it's easy to get used to being in a mess. I can see you're going to be a godsend to Tom.'

Jess's heart sank. Had she been brought here merely to tidy up after eccentric professors? Surely, she'd have been of more use being a plotter in an RAF station?

Remembering Miss Abernethy's criticism of Alice's constant complaints, Jess didn't question his words. If she got on with it until such time as she knew exactly what her role was, she could have a word with someone and ask for a transfer — although Miss Parker and Miss Abernethy had both mentioned that once someone was employed by Bletchley Park, that was where they would stay for the duration of the war.

But they couldn't keep her here if she wanted to leave — could they? In this topsy-turvy world, she suspected they could.

'Everything all right?' Louis asked.

'Ah!' she said, realising she'd been deep in thought and was frowning. 'Yes! It's just that I'm afraid of throwing the wrong thing away.'

That was true although she was more concerned with her future.

'I shouldn't worry,' Louis said. 'Tom'll soon let you know if you pick up something he wants.'

That seemed unlikely to Jess. Tom

was completely absorbed in what he was doing. How would he know what she was throwing away? He didn't seem aware that she or Louis were in the room with him.

'Right, if you don't mind taking the waste paper bin, I'll carry the crockery,' Louis said.

Jess looked at Tom for permission to go but he was arranging some long strips of thick cardboard on which were rows of letters, one beneath the other. Were they the rods he'd referred to earlier?

Following Jess's gaze, Louis said, 'Don't worry about Tom, he's following a train of thought and you won't get any sense out of him until it's time for rounders. And possibly not even then.' He winked at her and opened the door.

'I expect this all looks rather haphazard,' Louis said as they crossed the stable yard, 'but many of the most brilliant minds at Bletchley seem to thrive in chaos. Or perhaps it's more accurate to say they don't seem to be tuned in to things like the rest of us and work effectively despite the chaos. At least Tom was wearing suit trousers today. Last week, he turned up for work in pyjama top, bottoms and dressing gown.'

Jess laughed.

'Ah, that explains why I found a slipper on my chair! Is Tom the only person who works for you?'

'Good lord! He doesn't! I work for him!'

'But I thought you were his commanding officer,' Jess said. 'You seem to be . . . well . . . ' She tailed off feeling foolish for having jumped to conclusions based on their mode of dress.

'There aren't many commanding officers at Bletchley. Well, there are if you're a WAAF, I suppose. And the RAF people answer to someone. But by and large, the entire park is run a bit like a university with different departments collaborating. Tom works for Alan Turing who works with Dilly Knox. They both work with Gordon Welchman. And they're just a few of the dons we have here, and by no means the most important. I work in Alan's office and I'm more of a technician than boffin. Alan's brilliant, but often, I have to remind him to eat. When he gets something on his mind, he'll work for hours without food or sleep. There's so much going on in their minds, the normal things you and I take for granted like dressing and eating are often forgotten.

'One chap walks around the lake drinking tea and when he finishes, he throws the cup into the water. And there's Alan, who chains his mug to the radiator.' He nodded at the filthy cups, saucers and plates he was carrying. 'The people in the canteen go mad because there isn't enough money to replace crockery when it goes missing — but try telling Tom, Alan or Dilly that!' A tall, suited figure strode by, smoking a pipe. 'Good morning, Dorothy,' Louis said. 'May I introduce you to Tom's new assistant? Dorothy Whyte-Collins, this is Jessica Langley.'

'Pleased to meet you.' Dorothy had a high, rather squeaky voice and shook hands limply.

'Yes, before you ask, she is a woman,' Louis said, smiling at Jess's confusion, once Dorothy was out of earshot. 'She just prefers to wear men's clothing. She's a distinguished mathematician and is nowhere near as eccentric as some you'll find at Bletchley.'

Jess was shocked but tried not to show it. Men who threw cups in the lake, women who dressed as men and men who didn't bother to change out of their pyjamas in the morning weren't what she'd expected at all. It was like being trapped in *Alice In Wonderland*. Her father wouldn't approve.

Perhaps that was all the more reason to embrace this strange, new world. It was her world — even if she didn't understand it — and she didn't need his approval. It felt deliciously decadent.

★   ★   ★

Louis bought her tea and suggested they sat at a table while they drank.

'It'll give me a chance to fill you in a bit on the set-up here at Bletchley. Obviously, I can't be too specific but I can give you a general idea. The Park is ideally situated halfway between Oxford and Cambridge and dons have been recruited from both universities — mathematicians, linguists, classicists and of course veteran cryptanalysts from the last war, like Dilly. There are lots of other people here too and we're trying to find a way to intercept German messages and to use the intelligence to help us win the war.

'Easily said, but not so easily done because all the messages are encrypted and are just a jumble of letters. It's our job to decrypt them and find out what they say.'

'Ah!' For the first time, things started to make sense, with Tom poring over sheets of letters. 'But what do you do? Don't technicians usually work with machines?'

Louis beamed. 'Good question, Jess! Yes, I assist Alan with his Bombe Machines.'

'*Bomb* machines?'

'Bombe with an 'e', not 'bomb' as in explosives!' Louis smiled. 'But with any luck, our Bombe Machines will be more effective in bringing this war to a swift and final end than the sort of bomb we drop out of aircraft. The machines have been developed by Alan and Gordon to speed up the decryption of enemy messages. We've got a Bombe Machine in Hut 1 with more being built, and there's a team of people who operate them night and day. We've had a bit of luck so far, but the more Bombes we have, the faster we'll be able to decipher enemy messages.'

Machines that deciphered messages! Jess could not begin to imagine how that could be.

'Don't look so worried, Jess. I know things are a bit different at Bletchley but you'll soon find your feet.'

Jess shook her head. 'I'm not sure I will, Louis. I think there's been a dreadful mistake. I can't see how I fit into this world at all. Unless I've been brought here to clean up, of course. Everyone seems to have a special skill and know exactly what their job is, but I don't

71

belong. The Air Force trained me to be a plotter and I'm beginning to think I'd be better off going back to that.'

'I wasn't involved in your recruitment but I'm certain you weren't brought here as a cleaner. There must be some reason why you were invited to work here.'

'I won a crossword competition — '

'Ah! Well, that would be the reason.'

'Because I completed a crossword?'

'That wasn't any old crossword. It was a very tricky one.'

'How on earth do you know?'

'Because it was just one of the ways the top brass set out to recruit people to Bletchley. It was a strategy to find those who have the skills we need here without actually advertising. If you've been invited to work here, you fit the bill. Can you speak any foreign languages?'

'I can speak passable French and German — '

'Well, there you are! You're absolutely perfect!' Jess blushed. Louis drank his tea and watched her over the rim of his cup. His green eyes were framed with long, dark lashes and Jess felt her colour heighten under his scrutiny.

'Well,' he said, as he placed his cup on the saucer, 'we'd best get this back to Tom.' He picked up the third cup he'd bought for Tom.

'Won't it be cold?' Jess asked.

'Yes, but he won't mind. As you saw, when he's working on an idea, he's oblivious to what's going on around him. I could take him a cup of cod liver oil and he'd down it in one.'

Jess noticed that Louis's eyes crinkled at the corners when he smiled, which he did frequently.

He was funny, kind and empathetic, thought Jess. Good-looking too, in a quiet, unassuming sort of way. Not in the showy manner of many of the RAF pilots, with their devil-may-care attitude and flamboyant mannerisms. Louis's face, at first sight rather unremarkable, transformed when he became animated and especially when he smiled. Perhaps when he'd first come into the office, she'd been too agitated to take much in.

Now he'd given her an insight into the purpose of Bletchley Park and suggested a reason for her being there, she'd begun to relax and to notice things.

'. . . so, once we've taken Tom his tea, I'll show you around, introduce you to a few people. Oh, and I'll show you an Enigma Machine. Things'll make more sense once you see how that works.'

★ ★ ★

Tom accepted the tea and drank it without taking his eyes off the page of letters in front of him. Louis caught Jess's eye and, smiling conspiratorially, mouthed 'Cod liver oil.'

She stifled a giggle. They continued to clear Jess's desk and beneath several folders, they found a set of cardboard strips such as Tom had laid out on his desk which Louis told her were referred to as Dilly's Rods. After clearing the top, they dragged the desk towards the other window because Louis said the lighter it was, the easier it would be on her eyes.

'I'm just going to introduce Jess to Enigma and to Alan and Gordon if they're around,' Louis said and received a vague wave of the hand from Tom.

Jess followed him into one of the cottages which was slightly tidier than Tom's office had been earlier. It was empty and Louis dragged another chair to his desk for Jess, then placed a wooden box in front of her.

'This,' he said grandly, 'is an Enigma Machine. First used in 1923 by commercial banks to keep their communications secret, it was adopted by the German Navy and modified to make it even more secure. Shortly after, the Air Force and Army began to use them too.' He raised the lid of the box to reveal a keyboard similar to a typewriter's, but on the top were three rotating wheels and twenty-six small round windows, each marked with one letter of the alphabet.

'It looks very complicated.' Jess bit her lip.

'Not if you take it step by step. Now, I want you to imagine you're a private in the German Army and you've been asked to send a message. Firstly, you'll be told how to set the machine up, like this.' He rotated the wheels on the top and changed the plugs on the front.

'Now, you're going to encrypt the word 'Louis', so press the L key as if it were a typewriter.' Jess did as he'd asked. One of the tiny round windows lit up, illuminating the letter U. 'I'll make a note of that,' he said writing U on his pad. 'Now type the letter O.' As she tapped the O key, the letter D lit up on the top. Louis wrote D on his pad. 'Now continue with U, I and S and I'll note down the letters that light up on the top.'

She looked at what he'd written — *UDSBR.*

'Now, your next task would be to convert those letters to Morse Code and transmit them. The chap at the other end, would convert your Morse Code back into letters and then if his Enigma Machine was set to the same settings as yours, he'd type U D S B R into his machine, making a note of the illuminated letters on the

76

top of his machine. And guess what it would spell?'

'Louis!'

'Exactly!'

'You make it sound so simple!'

'Simple and elegant. And unfortunately for us, very difficult to break into. The settings on those three rotor wheels means that the number of combinations the machine can be set to is approximately fifteen million, million. And to make things even more complicated, the settings are always changed at midnight. So even if we knew the settings, we'd only have access to their messages for a few hours before they changed and we couldn't read them again.'

'It's like searching for a needle in a haystack,' Jess said.

'More like looking through a dozen haystacks for one needle. But luckily, we've had help from the Polish and the French who've done a lot of work on cracking the Enigma machines.'

'But surely with so many combinations, people are wasting their time trying to work out those letters?'

'It certainly looks like that but some-times there are ways of increasing the odds in our favour, especially if we have a crib.'

'Crib?'

'It's a sort of guess. Occasionally, the Germans use stock phrases for example, some operators finish their messages with *Heil Hitler*. It's sometimes possible to decipher the rest of the message by using intelligent guesswork and treat-ing it like a crossword puzzle where you already know a few of the letters. We had success with some Army and Air Force messages, and last June we found out the Luftwaffe was being refitted, which sug-gested they were about to take part in a major attack. Of course, now we know they were planning the Battle of Britain.

'We gained a good idea of German bomber strength from those decrypted messages and the top brass at the RAF were pleased to discover the Luftwaffe wasn't quite as strong as they'd assumed. And we had advance warning of certain air raids . . . You're frowning, Jess.'

'I was just remembering being at RAF Holsmere and how terrible it was during that time. It's hard to believe you were here at Bletchley intercepting Luftwaffe messages.'

'Yes, I suppose so. Sadly we've had no luck with the German Navy. Vice-Admiral Dönitz seems very wary and he's added layers of encryption to all Naval messages so we haven't made any headway at all. And while we struggle, his U-Boats sink our ships with ease. But hopefully, Alan and Gordon's Bombe Machines'll help us.'

'But when the Germans find out we're reading their messages, won't they simply make them more complicated?'

'If they knew we were reading their messages, yes. But it appears they don't. That's why everyone at Bletchley has to sign the Official Secrets Act.'

'But surely the Germans'll work it out, if they send messages to say they'll be somewhere at a certain time and our boys are there waiting?'

'The top brass go to great lengths to make it look as if we either learned any intelligence from a spy or we stumbled across it by accident. So, if we learned the location of a German battle cruiser, we'd send an aircraft over, making it look like it'd stumbled across the ship. Shortly after, bombers would attack. To the Germans, it would look as if we'd been lucky. In fact, it would've been planned meticulously. And it has to remain that way, or, as you say, the Germans will simply increase their security and we'll be locked out of all future communication.'

The door of the office flew open.

'Louis! Louis! Where are you?' A man hurried into the office and stopped when he saw Jess.

Louis leapt to his feet, 'Alan, this is our newest recruit, Jess Langley, Jess, this is Alan Turing.'

Alan nodded at Jess. 'Dilly's come up with a possible modification but we can't find a soldering iron. I think Tom's got them all but I can't get any sense out of him . . . ' He left the sentence hanging.

With an apologetic smile at Jess, Louis said, 'Duty calls. I'll come over to your office later and see how you're getting on. Perhaps we can have lunch together?'

He left with Alan, a soldering iron in each hand, and Jess returned to Tom's office.

'Ah, Miss . . . err,' Tom said as she entered, 'I do believe I owe you an apology. I'm afraid when you first arrived I was rather distracted. I imagine Louis has been showing you around?'

Tom spent the next few hours demonstrating how to use Dilly's Rods to help decipher messages. It was rather hit and miss but she quickly became accustomed to using them. Just as well, because once Tom had explained something, he moved on regardless of whether she'd understood. And often, he spoke to her in Latin. He explained he'd been a Professor of Egyptology at Cambridge University and had been recruited when Bletchley Park had first been set up. To Jess's relief after his earlier indifference, he now seemed quite engaging.

As promised, Louis returned in time for lunch and joined her and Tom in the bustling canteen. Afterwards, they gathered with a group of people on the lawn in front of the mansion.

'No, I'll just watch, thanks,' Jess said when she realised this was the rounders game that had been mentioned. She hadn't been very sporty at school and doubted she'd be able to hit the tennis ball with such a narrow bat. Louis explained it was a length of broom handle sawn to the right length, and with a hole in one end through which a leather strap had been threaded.

'Where are the posts?' Jess asked.

This was a question which seemed to be generating heated debate, much of it in Latin.

'Generally, they use trees but there's often a bit of disagreement about which trees,' he said. 'Yesterday that coniferous tree was the third post but the day before, it was that oak to its right.'

But despite the argument still raging, several tweed-jacketed men had already begun to play and groups of young women wandered over to watch.

'I say! Super batting!' one of the women called out as a tall, bespectacled man hit the ball, flung down the bat and loped across to the conifer — his pipe firmly clamped in his mouth.

It occurred to Jess she really ought to try to sort out her billet before the end of the day, but the thought of expressing her discontent to Mrs Grady wasn't anywhere near as appealing as sitting on the grass next to Louis, watching the ridiculous rounders game and being introduced to Louis's friends as they sauntered past.

Surely it was better not to fuss and to get to know a few people. Perhaps she'd overreacted about the billet anyway, egged on by Alice's dissatisfaction. She'd give it another try tonight and persuade Alice to do the same. After all, Mrs Grady hadn't been expecting them yesterday, so it wasn't surprising she'd been grouchy.

As for sharing a bed . . . well, perhaps

Jess could sleep on the couch downstairs if Mrs Grady didn't mind. She was shorter than Alice, who'd have the double bed to herself. That would please her.

The game ended with another argument about who was actually on whose team but it was half-hearted, and groups of men and women wandered off back to the mansion or their huts. Tom gave Jess a pile of messages to practise on with her set of Dilly's Rods. She spent the afternoon working, although she didn't make any headway in deciphering anything and she didn't see Tom again that afternoon to ask for help. But at least she felt more at home than when she'd arrived that morning.

There was no sign of Alice as Jess walked home. Perhaps she was working late. Jess had been afraid of getting lost but she soon realised the tall chimney belching out smoke behind Brick Lane would guide her to number sixteen.

Turn a negative into a positive. Jess was proud of herself. She'd chosen to view the chimney which was discharging evil-smelling smoke over the houses below, as a beacon guiding her home, rather than an aggravation.

'Oh, it's you,' Mrs Grady said when she opened the door. 'Well, you'd better join your friend upstairs. Leave the room as tidy as you found it. And hurry up with your packing. My Frank'll be home soon and he'll be expecting 'is dinner, so I'd appreciate it if you'd be gone as soon as possible.'

'Gone?'

'Yes. You and Miss Hoity-Toity.'

'Are you throwing us out?' Jess asked.

'No. Your friend said she was leaving.'

Alice appeared at the top of the stairs with her suitcase.

'Ah, Jess. I'm moving out. I've got a place in a hostel. Did you manage to get another billet today?'

'No, I . . . '

'So you're not leaving?' Mrs Grady asked Jess.

'No. . . '

'Well, I wish you'd bloomin' make up

your mind! I'd better set another place at the table,' she said and stomped into the kitchen.

'Why didn't they sort a new billet out for you today?' Alice asked.

'Well . . . I . . . I didn't actually ask. I was rather busy,' she added, knowing the excuse sounded unconvincing.

Alice snorted. 'If you've got any sense, you'll move out as soon as you can. That thieving landlady took my bar of chocolate. And I'm sure she'd been through my things. I'd check nothing's missing from your stuff when you go up.'

'Surely not!'

'Oh, Jess, grow up! If you don't mind me saying, you seem rather naïve. Go into Bletchley tomorrow and tell them you demand a new room. They weren't too happy but I stood my ground until they found me a place. The fact is, if you allow people to treat you like a doormat, they'll wipe their feet all over you. Well — good luck.'

She strode down the street, back straight and head high, confident of her place in the world.

Jess ran upstairs. Surely, Alice had been wrong about Mrs Grady taking her chocolate and going through her things.

Jess surveyed her possessions. She hadn't left much out — just her hairbrush, an alarm clock and a torch. The other things had been arranged in the bottom drawer, the one Alice had allocated her after taking the top one for herself.

Everything was where Jess had left it, although it was hard to tell if someone had merely lifted items, looked beneath and then replaced them.

She pulled Gibby's jewellery box from the rear corner of the drawer and opened it, her heart pounding. What would she do if the pearls were gone? But they were still there. She put them on, slipping them inside her uniform blouse and determined to keep them on, just in case.

★ ★ ★

'My Frank won't be back till later, so it's just us two women,' Mrs Grady said when Jess sat down at the kitchen table for dinner. 'Now, how was your first day at work?'

Was the landlady trying to make up for her earlier rudeness?

'Fine, thanks.'

'Good. And what did you do?'

An innocent question but Jess knew she must not answer truthfully.

'Nothing exciting. Just filing, that sort of thing.'

Mrs Grady ladled stew on to Jess's plate.

'So what sort of place is Bletchley Park? A few years ago, it was a private house. My friend, Minnie, worked in the kitchen, so I heard all about the Leon family. And then they sold up and left. And then … ' She paused dramatically. 'There's been all sorts of comings and goings with all manner of strange people. There are lots of whispers about what they do in there. So, I wondered what's actually goin' on.'

'I'm not really sure,' Jess said.

'You must know something.' Mrs Grady's friendliness was being replaced by irritation.

'Not really. I worked on my own most of the day, filing. Although . . . ' she said as if about to impart a secret.

'Yes?' said Mrs Grady, her spoon paused halfway from the plate to her mouth.

'I did some typing.' Jess wanted to smile at the disappointment in the landlady's face. Typing obviously wasn't what she wanted to hear about.

'I'm quite good at typing. I was the fastest in the class and I can reach up to ninety words per minute,' Jess continued.

As she hoped, the prospect of a discussion about her typing speed quelled any further questioning from Mrs Grady.

Jess helped to wash the dishes and tidy away, then feigning tiredness, she went to her bedroom to escape more questioning.

The single lightbulb was so dim in the bedroom that wherever Jess sat with her book, she seemed to throw a shadow over the pages, making it hard to read until she eventually fell asleep. She woke hours later and checked her clock. It was twenty past one and her feet were freezing.

But it wasn't the cold which had woken her. There'd been a noise outside her door. Someone breathing heavily. Probably Mrs Grady or her husband having just climbed the stairs.

A man softly cleared his throat and she knew it wasn't the landlady. Jess sat up and listened, her heart hammering. Mr Grady was still there, breathing heavily outside her door. A floorboard creaked and the door handle grated as it turned.

'Who's there?' Jess called, her voice almost a squeak.

The door handle stopped moving although she could still hear the heavy breathing.

'Hello!' she said, picking up her torch and shining it at the door.

Heavy footsteps moved away across the landing. Jess leapt out of bed and dragged the chest of drawers across the opening of the door.

She switched the light on and climbed back into bed. There was no possibility of her going back to sleep now — her heart was beating wildly.

She tried to make sense of what had happened. Perhaps Mr Grady had been drunk and mistaken her room for his? But then why hadn't he simply lurched in, rather than skulking about outside the door, breathing heavily and slowly turning the handle as if trying to do it silently?

Whatever the reason, it made up Jess's mind. She wouldn't sleep one more night in this house. In fact, there was no point waiting for the morning. She'd get up now, pack and leave. If no room could be found for her, then she'd sleep in Tom's office — on the floor, if necessary. But she wouldn't spend another night under this roof.

It didn't take long to pack her belongings but as she went to the door, she wondered if Mr Grady would wake up and come out of his bedroom. Or suppose Mrs

Grady heard her and wanted to know what she was doing, stealing out like a thief? She could hardly tell the landlady her husband had tried to get in her room and . . .

And what? She suspected it would all be explained away as a mistake and Jess would look like a hysterical fool.

She turned the door handle slowly, stopping each time it began to squeal until finally the door was open. Then she crept downstairs and quietly let herself out into the dark and silent street. Once outside, she walked away from number sixteen as quickly as she could, her breath billowing behind her in the chilly, night air.

★ ★ ★

Jess was asleep at her desk, her head resting on her arms, when Tom and Louis arrived.

'That's what I call dedication! Have you been here all night?' Louis' smile slipped when he saw Jess's suitcase.

'Where are you going?'

'I don't know,' Jess admitted. She moved her head from side to side to ease the stiffness and tried to wiggle her fingers.

'Tea!' Louis decided. 'Then you can tell me all about it.'

They looked at Tom to see if he minded them disappearing to the canteen. He was kneeling on the floor, rifling through a pile of papers.

'Tea for me, please. Toast'd be good too,' he said without looking up.

'Did he threaten you?' Louis asked when Jess told him about Mr Grady's night-time attempt to enter her room.

'No, he didn't say anything. I shouted out before he actually came in.'

'So, it's possible he made a mistake . . .'

'Anything's possible but if he was simply going to bed, I don't know why he stood outside what he thought was his bedroom for so long and then tried to creep in.'

'Perhaps he'd had an argument with

his wife and was nervous she'd kick him out of the bedroom … '

Jess looked down at her tea. Had she been too hasty? Perhaps there'd been an innocent explanation. She began to wonder if she'd completely overreacted. But now she'd walked out of Mrs Grady's house, she couldn't go back.

'Was there a lock on your bedroom door?' Louis asked.

Jess shook her head. She was beginning to feel sick. What would the people in the billet office say when they realised she'd simply walked out of her billet in the middle of the night?

'Well, if you were anxious, that's enough for me. No one should be afraid in their billet. Let's go to the office and see what they can do,' Louis said, patting her hand. 'Don't worry, I'm sure they'll find you something.'

My life's full of ghosts, suspicions half-truths and shadows, Jess thought, there's nothing substantial to battle against.

★ ★ ★

'Do you realise how hard it is to come by rooms, young lady?' Miss Gordon said. She tapped a staccato beat on the desk with her pen. 'And you want a new room, all because the gentleman of the house accidentally took a wrong turn?'

'I don't think it was accidental,' Jess said although now, she wasn't convinced herself and she could see Miss Gordon didn't believe her.

'And did you do or say anything to Mr Grady, to give him the impression you might welcome a visit to your room during the night?'

'No! I never met him. I've only been there two nights.'

Miss Gordon's eyebrows rose in disbelief.

'So, let me get this straight. You've never met the gentleman. He might not even know you're in his house and when he tries to go into your room in the middle of the night, you immediately assume you're under threat?'

Jess looked down and nodded.

'Grady... Grady,' Miss Gordon said,

95

pushing her pen into her frizzy hair and scratching her head, 'Isn't she the woman in Brick Lane? A very rude girl was in here yesterday complaining about her. Miss Watson, no, Wilson. Miss Wilson,' she said rolling her eyes to the ceiling.

Jess sighed. She was about to be grouped together with Alice, who'd already made an unfavourable impression.

'Alice and I only met the day before yesterday when we arrived and we were billeted together. She didn't like the fact we had to share a bed.'

'Yes, she told me — several times. And she accused the landlady of stealing chocolate from her. I expect she ate it herself and then forgot. But in all fairness, you shouldn't have had to share a bed. That's why we immediately found her a new place in a hostel.'

'Would it, perhaps, be possible for me to join her in the hostel?' Jess asked politely, trying to divorce herself from Alice's approach of demanding satisfaction.

'No, I'm sorry, Miss Wilson had the

last place. You wouldn't believe the trouble I'm having finding billets. Every day new staff arrive and I'm expected to wave a magic wand and find places for people to stay! It's just not possible. And then, there are the moaners and the complainers like your friend who come in here and raise their voices at me.' She looked accusingly at Jess.

'I'm really sorry, Miss Gordon, but I'm desperate.'

'Well, whose fault is that? I'm afraid you'll just have to wait until I can place you somewhere.'

The door opened and Phyllis, the girl from the Mechanised Transport Corps who'd given Jess and Alice a lift to work the previous morning, entered clutching a folder. A delicious floral perfume wafted in with her, masking the dusty, musty smell of the room.

'I've got a few more, Miss Gordon,' she said as she placed the folder on the desk and turned to go. Then, recognising Jess, she stopped.

'Jessica, isn't it? Is everything all right?'

'Miss Langley has very foolishly vacated her billet without having secured another place first,' Miss Gordon said, opening the folder.

'I'm not surprised,' said Phyllis. 'It was positively ghastly. And that dragon of a landlady...'

'Oh,' said Miss Gordon, 'do you know of her?'

'Know of her? I met her yesterday! What an appalling woman ... Anyway, so sorry to interrupt but I thought you might like that list immediately.' Phyllis left, and the perfume faded and was gone.

Miss Gordon looked at Jess with more sympathetic eyes. 'There might be something suitable for you in this,' she said tapping the folder with her pen. 'It's a list of potential billets. Anyway, I'll let you know.'

Jess thanked her and turned to go. She was sure Alice would have insisted something be found for her before she left the office, but Jess was aware she hadn't done any work so far. She'd go back to the stable yard and return to Miss Gordon at lunchtime — although she was dreading it.

Why do I find it so hard to stand up for myself?

Phyllis was waiting in the corridor outside.

'Did Miss Gordon sort you out with accommodation?' she asked.

Jess shook her head, 'No. I'll pop back at lunch time and see if she's found anything.'

She forced herself to sound upbeat.

'Well, she jolly well should find you something amongst all those new people I've found her. Commander Denniston asked me last night if I could help with the shortage of billets. Daddy knows several people in the area and I've spent ages telephoning his friends and contacts, trying to find some more places. I came up with some good ones, too.' She paused and frowned, 'Actually, I've got an idea. Don't bother going back to see Miss Gordon. I'll come by and pick you up tonight. I'm living with my aunt just outside Bletchley at the moment. There're a few of us girls staying there. But there's room for another.'

'Really? Won't your aunt mind?'

'No. She's a great sport. Stay the night and see what you think.'

* * *

'You look much happier, Jess,' Louis said when he came into Tom's office at lunchtime. 'Does that mean you've got somewhere to stay?'

'Yes, and what's more, I found a crib in one of the German messages! Tom's gone over to the Bombe Machines.'

'Well done. What did you find?'

'I found the word *Wetterbericht* — weather report — at the beginning of a message.'

Having found a compound word and its position in the message gave an enormous clue to the way the Enigma Machines had been set up in Germany that day. Using what Jess had discovered would allow the programmes, which were known as menus, to be set up on the Bombe Machines and with any luck, all the messages received encrypted with the day's settings would be decrypted and the information collected.

At midnight, the Enigma settings would be changed and the messages once again scrambled but at least that day's messages would have been read — if the Bombes could find the settings.

'Right, let's celebrate! A ham sandwich and cup of tea in the canteen and a game of rounders after!' Louis said. 'Does life get any better?' He caught her hand and twirled her as if they were dancing. 'By the way, now you're an old hand at Bletchley, perhaps you'd like to join the Scottish Dancing Society. I belong. It's great fun. We meet tomorrow night. And the Chess Club meets the following night. I bet you're good at chess!'

He still held her hand and Jess twirled again. After such a frightening start to her day and the initial self-recrimination at making herself homeless, it was all starting to work out perfectly.

She smiled at Louis.

How had she not noticed how handsome he was when she first met him? But more importantly, he was kind and caring.

The day was wonderful and so was Louis.

He was right, life couldn't possibly be better.

3

Tom and Dilly were in a heated discussion when Jess returned from the rounders game after lunch. The match had finished when the captains of both sides failed to agree on the rules, which seemed to change according to who was scoring.

'You have to go around the trees to score a rounder!'

'Nonsense! You only need touch the trunks with the bat!' Gradually, people drifted back to work, deep in conversation.

Although she'd been with Miss Gordon trying to arrange accommodation, Tom hadn't remarked on her not starting work. In fact, he hadn't seemed to notice her absence at all. He had, however, been excited when she'd found the crib and immediately rushed off to show Alan.

She'd brought him several cups of

tea and ensured he had a sandwich for lunch, although he'd only eaten half of it until she reminded him he still had food on his plate.

It was rather like babysitting a precocious child. However, the office was much tidier and he'd grunted in surprise when she'd immediately brought him a report he suddenly decided he needed. She'd only just filed it away so she knew exactly where it was, but it was unlikely he'd have known that. It was early days, but she could see how she might fit into this world and be useful.

She was ready and waiting when Phyllis strode into the office at the end of her shift. Tom looked up as a chilly breeze wafted in carrying the floral notes of her perfume. He immediately looked down and carried on muttering over a large circuit diagram.

Phyllis grinned at Jess. She was obviously used to such eccentricity.

'Ready?' she asked.

'I'm off, Tom. See you tomorrow,' Jess said.

He raised a hand without taking his eyes off his finger, which was tracing one of the lines on the diagram.

Phyllis led her unerringly through the blackness to the parking area near the gate, negotiating pot holes and bumps. Jess could see two figures already waiting by the shooting brake.

'Let Edna go in the front seat,' Phyllis whispered, 'she makes an awful fuss if she doesn't get her own way.'

'This is Jessica Langley, the girl I told you about,' she called as she approached the two girls. Then turning to Jess, 'Edna Houghton.' She gestured to the girl hovering near the passenger door. 'And Gwen Armstrong.' She waved her hand at the other girl.

'Court,' Edna said.

'Armstrong!' Gwen and Phyllis said together and both laughed. Gwen shook Jess's hand.

'My surname's actually Armstrong-Court but it's such a dreadful mouthful, I've decided to drop the Court. I might pick it up again after the war.' Her laugh was infectious.

'If I had a double-barrelled surname, I wouldn't drop part of it to please anyone,' Edna said haughtily.

'Ah well, it takes all sorts,' said Phyllis, unlocking the car doors. 'Now, hop in. I've been driving about all day and I'd like a rest.'

Once in the car, no one talked about work. Gwen and Phyllis chatted about the forthcoming drama group Christmas Revue, discussing members of the cast until Edna suddenly cut in, 'I say, have you forgotten to drop off Janet?'

'I think you mean Jessica, and she's coming to Lestcombe with us.'

'Oh, I see.' After a moment's thought, Edna added, 'You mean she's staying the night with us?' Her tone suggested the prospect was rather inappropriate.

'No,' said Phyllis and Edna grunted with satisfaction. 'I mean she's staying the night with my uncle and aunt and in fact, if she likes it, a lot longer than that.'

'Oh, I see,' Edna said quickly.

Gwen silently patted Jess's hand. She'd

turned her face towards Jess but it was too dark to read her expression. Nevertheless, Jess knew she was trying to make up for Edna's obvious dissatisfaction at their new roommate. It was apparent from the three girls' accents they came from the upper class and perhaps Edna had judged Jess and found her wanting. Her middle-class accent would have given her away.

Jess lowered her head, recalling how she'd judged Kitty when she'd met her at RAF Holsmere. Unless you looked past Kitty's wantonness, you wouldn't see the generosity of spirit — and she hadn't done until it was almost too late.

Gwen was in mid-chorus, singing one of the songs to be performed in the Christmas Revue when Phyllis turned off the lane into a large drive.

'The gates are gone,' she said by way of explanation. 'They were wrought iron, you know. Uncle Reginald gave them up for the war effort. He was so upset.'

The car crunched on gravel and drew up in front of an enormous house, silver in the moonlight.

Edna, Gwen and Jess got out while Phyllis drove around the house to the garages at the back.

'It's much nicer than Bletchley Mansion, isn't it?' said Gwen.

'Bletchley!' Edna scoffed. 'Bletchley is utterly hideous! It looks as if someone's stolen all sorts of bits from other buildings and stuck them together at random. It's an architectural mongrel! I expect the family who owned it had more money than sense — and certainly no taste. New money, I wouldn't wonder. That's what happens when people from the lower classes try to pass themselves off as their betters — '

'Well,' said Gwen quickly, cutting off Edna's denunciation of the lower classes, 'I rather like Bletchley. It's unusual. And interesting.'

It was obvious to Jess, even in the moonlight, that Lestcombe Hall was the height of style and good taste — and completely different from Bletchley. She was grateful that Gwen had tried to protect her from Edna's snobbery but it was obvious that if they were all to be likened to a building, she would be the mismatched mansion at Bletchley with what Edna thought of as its pretentions at grandeur. Phyllis, Edna and Gwen would all be like elegant Lestcombe Hall.

The grand front door opened. It was Phyllis.

'I came in the back way to open the door, rather than disturb Morrison,' she said as they all filed into the grand entrance hall.

Phyllis took Jess up the curved staircase to her bedroom. 'I'm afraid you'll be responsible for keeping it clean,' she said apologetically. 'All the maids have gone. Auntie Beatrice only has Morrison, the butler, Mrs Jenner, the cook, and Willis, the gardener. Everyone else left at the beginning of the war.'

'Of course,' said Jess. 'I don't expect anyone to wait on me. I'm used to looking after myself.'

Phyllis was silent for a few moments.

'Look, Jessica, I know Edna can be

a bally awful snob at times but I hope you won't let it upset you. Some people refuse to accept change. But the whole world's changing — and that's a good thing. People like Edna will cling on to the last, trying to maintain the status quo. But it's obvious from Bletchley that things work better when people cooperate regardless of distinctions.

'We're all contributing what we can and it seems to be working. And if it doesn't work — well, I suppose we'll all be under Herr Hitler's heel and our class system won't mean a bean anyway.' She put a hand on Jess's shoulder. 'So please ignore Edna. You're very welcome here and I'm sure Auntie Beatrice will think so too.'

Jess smiled. It was kind of Phyllis, if worrying that she hadn't yet actually asked her aunt.

'So, I'll leave you to freshen up and come back in twenty minutes and take you down to the kitchen. We usually eat supper there during the week. Oh, and Auntie's hosting a fund-raising ball on

Saturday — not along the lines of what she'd once have held at Lestcombe, but you're invited.'

Jess gasped.

'Have you other arrangements?' Phyllis asked.

'It's just that I've never been to a ball and I've nothing to wear — only my uniform. Is it all right if I just stay in my room?'

'Certainly not! You shall go, Cinderella!'

★ ★ ★

After supper, the girls went upstairs and once Edna had gone into her room, Gwen invited Jess into hers. Phyllis appeared minutes later with a pale blue silk dress. She held it up.

'What do you think?' she asked.

'It's beautiful!' Jess said. 'Is that what you're going to wear on Saturday?'

'Me? No. I'm afraid it's torn.' Phyllis held the dress so that the two girls could see the flounce at the bottom. 'I was dancing with a clumsy oaf at my last ball and he trod on the bottom. It tore. He was mortified, poor man.'

'Can't Mrs Jenner mend it?' Gwen asked. 'She's a whizz with a sewing machine.'

'She said she'd have a go, but it'll mean cutting off some of the flounce because of the way it's torn. It'll be too short for me. However . . . ' She held it up in front of Jess. 'You're so much shorter than me, I'm sure if Mrs Jenner cut the flounce off, hemmed the bottom and perhaps took the bodice in slightly, it would fit you perfectly.'

'Me?' Jess's mouth fell open. The dress was gorgeous. If the alterations were done as Phyllis suggested, Jess could see the skirt would still drape beautifully. But it was the top of the dress which worried her. It had a princess bodice with puff sleeves and would display more flesh than she'd ever shown before.

Her father's disapproving face flashed into her mind. She knew exactly what he'd say.

'So, what d'you think?' Phyllis asked

in a worried tone. 'You aren't angry with me for suggesting it, are you?'

'No, no! Not at all! The dress is beautiful. And you're so kind.'

But dare she wear such a dress?

Why not? Other girls wore gowns like this.

'It's wonderful and I'd be thrilled to wear it. Thank you,' she said warmly.

'Right, slip it on and we'll get Mrs Jenner to pin it up. No time like the present,' Phyllis said briskly, handing her the dress.

Mrs Jenner promised to have it ready for the ball and offered to make a stole out of what was left of the flounce. 'It won't keep you warm, dear, but it'll look quite stylish,' she said.

It'll cover me up a bit too, Jess thought in relief.

'Shoes,' said Phyllis. 'Let's see what you've got to go with the dress.'

Other than Jess's sensible, black WAAF lace-ups, she had a pair of silver sandals she'd worn once. Genevieve had persuaded her to buy them for the one occasion she accompanied her house-mates to a dance. She had remained at their table all night, despite the others' efforts to persuade her to join them on the dance floor.

There was a good reason — she couldn't dance. Her parents had not approved of dancing. Modesty at all times, her father had preached and without rationalising it, Jess had absorbed his message, finding the thought of a man holding her close and their bodies moving in rhythm, rather improper.

She held the silver sandals up, dangling them by their straps, and stared at them doubtfully.

'What's the matter with them?' asked Gwen. 'Don't they fit?'

'Yes — but I might wear my uniform shoes.'

'No!' Gwen and Phyllis said together.

'It's not as if I'll be dancing, so no one will see,' Jess said, defensively.

'Won't be dancing? What nonsense!' Phyllis said. 'You bally well will be dancing, my girl!'

Gwen placed her hand on Jess's arm.

'What's wrong?'

Jess didn't feel she could refuse to tell them.

'I can't dance.'

'Is that all?' said Phyllis when Jess explained, 'You've got days to learn!'

'And I know the perfect teacher,' Gwen said.

'We'll ask Louis Gresham.'

Gwen, it transpired, knew Louis because she worked in another of the cottages in the stable yard with Dilly and some other girls. Collectively, Phyllis revealed, they had been dubbed 'Dilly's Fillies'.

'It's utter poppycock that Dilly chose us for our looks and not our brains!' Gwen said crossly.

'But you can see people's point,' said the practical Phyllis. 'It looks rather improbable that he chose such a bunch of good-looking girls based merely on their intelligence.'

'It might look improbable but it's true! I've never met so many clever women,'

Gwen said. 'Dilly likes women. But not like that!' she added when Phyllis rolled her eyes. 'He respects us. And he says we work harder and more systematically than men. Anyway, I've seen you going in and out of the bungalow opposite our cottage, Jess, so I'm guessing you're working with Tom Kemp.'

Jess frowned. She knew she wasn't supposed to discuss work.

'It's all right,' said Gwen, guessing why she was so worried. 'If you're working for Tom, then you and I are on the same team. We don't have to discuss work, but it's all right to know where each other spends their time.'

'So, you know Louis too?' Jess asked.

'Oh, most people know Louis!' Gwen said. 'He works with Alan Turing, next door to us and he's often in and out of our office, discussing things with Dilly. Phyllis knows him because we all belong to the Drama Group — and we're all in the Christmas Revue this year.'

'Perhaps you'll join?' Gwen said. 'We're a bit short in the chorus . . . You can sing, can't you?'

'Well . . . ' Jess had been told she had a lovely voice by other members of the St Margaret's Church Choir but when someone had suggested to the vicar that she sang a solo, he'd refused and when the pianist had broken a finger, Rev Langley had insisted Jess take over on the piano. Her father had always found a reason for her not to sing in the choir after that.

'I'm not sure I'd be any good,' she said.

'One thing at a time,' said Phyllis. 'The most pressing thing is to at least be able to waltz by Saturday.'

'I'll ask Louis tomorrow,' said Gwen.

Jess was grateful they didn't expect her to arrange her own dancing lessons with Louis because she knew she wasn't bold enough to ask him . . . nor willing to take the risk he'd refuse.

★ ★ ★

'Five more minutes,' Jess shouted through the door when Phyllis knocked and asked if she was ready to go downstairs. She made her voice sound breathless, as if inside her bedroom, there was a whirl of activity.

There wasn't. She was dressed, sitting on her bed, staring at the floor.

Gwen had pinned up her curls in a sophisticated style and then with a warning to Jess not to disturb it as she put her dress on, she'd rushed off to get herself ready.

Now, Gwen and Edna were downstairs waiting for the guests who would start arriving shortly.

'Do you need some help?' Phyllis called.

'No!' Jess shouted in panic. 'Thank you, I'm nearly ready. I'm just putting my shoes on,' she added, hoping Phyllis hadn't noticed her abruptness.

She looked down at the sandals she was supposed to be putting on. They'd been on her feet for the last thirty minutes.

What was wrong with her? It should have been simple. She'd been invited to a ball. A ball was an enjoyable occasion.

Her partner would be Louis. She liked Louis — a lot. So, what was the problem and why couldn't she relax and look forward to the evening?

There were several reasons and she tried to deal with each one in a logical manner.

Firstly, it was hard to ignore the guilt planted and nurtured by her father. It was a ball. It would be frivolous and indecent, with women wearing gowns such as her own which showed off shoulders and chests.

She was gradually tackling the prejudices and influence her father had instilled in her. The first step was to recognise them, and then to ignore them resolutely — despite the twinges of conscience she felt when she did so.

There is nothing wrong with a ball — especially this one, which will raise money for war widows and orphans. There is nothing wrong in showing your shoulders and this is a beautiful gown. She pulled the sheer stole Mrs Jenner had made her tighter, and ensured the brooch was secure.

Secondly, and harder to rationalise, she knew she was going to make a complete fool of herself in front of so many well-connected people. How well-connected, she'd only learned the previous week. Phyllis wasn't simply Miss Briggs, she was the Honourable Phyllis Briggs and likewise, Edna was the Honourable Edna Houghton. As for Gwen, who seemed the most down to earth, she was Lady Gwendolyn Armstrong-Court.

'They're all Debs,' Louis had told her. 'Debutantes,' he added when she'd looked mystified. 'You know, aristocratic young ladies who are presented at Court. Girls in Pearls.'

Jess had never heard the term 'Girls in Pearls' but she'd read about Debs. It hadn't, however, occurred to her she'd be mixing with them, much less that they'd be happy to mix with her. And what's more, she was living with them.

When Jess had first met Phyllis, Gwen and Edna, their accents had given their class away — and the fact that Phyllis's uncle lived in a mansion, of course. But at Bletchley, everyone appeared to be treated the same. The goal was to outwit the enemy by breaking their codes, not to sustain the social hierarchy. People were judged on their intellect rather than their family's wealth.

Phyllis and Gwen certainly hadn't made an issue of Jess's lowlier status and when she'd asked Gwen why Phyllis had suggested she move in with them, Gwen had replied, 'Because you needed a room,' as if it were as simple as that.

When she'd persisted and asked why she and Phyllis were so kind, Gwen had seemed puzzled.

'Why wouldn't we be? We're all working as a team. No one at Bletchley cares about your background. It's how things should be.'

Not an opinion shared by everyone, Jess knew, from several of Edna's barbed remarks. But it was comforting, nonetheless. And now, she was about to humiliate herself among people who might or might not accept her as one of them.

But third on her list of reasons to dread the evening was the one which bothered her most. Louis.

Gwen had asked him if he'd teach Jess to dance and he'd readily agreed. After their shifts had finished, he'd taught her to waltz. She was surprised at how easy it was to dance with Louis, and she'd also almost mastered the foxtrot.

Seeing how well they danced together, Gwen suggested Louis accompany Jess to the ball.

He'd seemed rather surprised but he'd agreed. On one hand, Jess was appalled that he'd been manoeuvred into spending an evening with her. But on the other, her heart beat faster when she imagined them dancing together — until common sense warned her it was unlikely he'd stay with her all evening.

Why should he? It's not as if he's asked me out on a date.

'Jess! Come on! People will be arriving soon!' Phyllis was knocking on her door again.

Jess sighed, got up and opened the door.

'Good heavens,' Phyllis exclaimed. 'Did someone die? Look at you! Anyone'd think you were on your way to a funeral! This evening's going to be fun! Pull your shoulders back. Put a smile on your face. And . . . ' She stopped and sniffed the air. 'No. That's not right. Wait there.'

Jess was horrified. She'd bathed and washed her hair. What could Phyllis have smelled that had made her frown like that?

'Arms out,' Phyllis said when she returned. 'No, not like that!' as Jess held her arms out sideways. 'Like this!' She placed her wrists together, palms up. In her hand was a bottle shaped like a female torso covered in flowers.

Jess placed her wrists together and Phyllis took the stopper out of the bottle, immediately releasing a cloud of perfume — the same perfume which accompanied Phyllis everywhere.

'Do I smell?' Jess whispered, too embarrassed to say the words aloud.

'No,' said Phyllis, 'not yet.' She dabbed the stopper to Jess's wrists and then bent to sniff them. 'That's better! There's never an occasion when Schiaparelli's Shocking isn't appropriate. Now you're dressed.'

★ ★ ★

'That gown suits you much better than it did me,' Phyllis commented. 'I looked quite washed out in it. But it really suits you.'

Jess had never worn anything so sumptuous. Mrs Jenner had adjusted it to perfection and now, as Jess walked across the ballroom floor with Phyllis, she shivered with delight as the silky fabric caressed her skin. It fitted perfectly over her curves and draped sensuously around her legs as she walked.

Louis was one of the first to arrive. Usually very smart, he was now dressed impeccably and he complimented her on her appearance.

How poised he was! And how easily he fitted into any occasion, his self-confidence seeming to be enough for the both of them.

He offered to bring her some punch but she'd decided not to touch any alcohol. Whereas it might have given her courage, she knew from experience, having once been persuaded by Kitty to sample some cocktails, it limited her balance and co-ordination. And tonight, she needed to ensure she remained upright and in control.

Louis brought her a glass of cordial and chatted to her in the natural way he did when they were at work. Gradually she began to relax and when the music began, he guided her gently onto the dance floor, whispering encouragement in her ear.

Having such a partner made it easy and she found she was dancing without having to think about what her feet were doing. Several of the young women who didn't have partners glanced at Louis longingly but he stayed with her, generously ensuring that whatever he did, he nurtured the illusion she had frequented balls and other such gatherings all her life.

* * *

Jess lay in bed, her knees drawn up and her hands under her head. The fragrance Phyllis had dabbed on her wrists earlier enveloped her in its floral perfume. Shocking, Phyllis had called it — Shocking by Schiaparelli. How appropriate.

The entire evening had been shocking.

Not in a bad way. It had been simply marvellous. But shocking nonetheless because all her concerns and uncertainties had turned out to be completely unfounded. The disaster she'd anticipated had been a wonderful experience.

Rev Langley's values which Jess had unconsciously absorbed melted away during the evening. Everyone had behaved with the utmost decorum and the sight of so many ladies with bare shoulders and décolletage blunted her embarrassment at her own lack of modesty. What was the point in covering up when the majority of women were showing just as much flesh? Jess wondered, and she'd removed the gauzy stole. Before long, it felt completely normal and she was pleased that Gibby's lovely pearls had been shown off to advantage.

'You really are one of the Girls in Pearls now!' Louis had whispered to her. She'd blushed under his scrutiny, although she knew he wasn't looking at her but at the pearls.

She'd worried she'd show herself up, but Louis had somehow steered her through each situation as it arose, making everything easy. If anyone had noticed her lack of class, no one had remarked on it or made her feel inadequate.

Louis had been amazing. She sighed and felt a warm glow radiate throughout her body. It was hard to believe he'd not strayed from her side all evening. How wonderful to have clasped hands while they danced, and to have felt his fingers resting lightly on her back. His touch had been deferential and respectful. And as every minute passed, she'd become more certain she was falling in love with him.

But the most shocking thing about the entire evening was that she'd actually longed for him to hold her tightly and pull her to him, then to kiss her deeply and passionately. She gasped at the picture her imagination conjured up, never having experienced the sensations which filled her body.

But if her evening with its unexpected success and the unfamiliarity and boldness of her feelings had all combined to shock her, the end of the evening had been quite an anti-climax. After Louis's considerate behaviour towards her, she'd assumed he shared her feelings and she'd expected — well, hoped, anyway — that he'd lead her somewhere out of the way of prying eyes, hold her in his arms and kiss her.

But she'd been disappointed when

he'd merely taken her hand and kissed it before saying goodbye and leaving with a smile.

He was the perfect gentleman, Jess thought wistfully, wishing he'd not been quite so well-behaved.

4

Daniel Matthews knew his boss was angry because he was grinding his teeth. He recognised the slight movement of the jaw and of course, the scowl which brought Mr Bullock's heavy, dark brows together over narrowed eyes.

There was no need for anger, Daniel reflected. Just because the two Wrens opposite him in the railway carriage were staring at him, giggling like schoolgirls and trying to catch his eye, didn't mean he was interested in them. Mr Bullock had expressly warned him there would be dozens of girls at Bletchley Park and they were all off-limits. That was fine by him.

'If you can't behave yerself, I'll find another assistant,' he'd said when he told Daniel he'd be accompanying him on a business trip to Bletchley.

The British Tabulating Machine

Company Ltd was situated in Letchworth, Hertfordshire, about thirty miles from Bletchley and Daniel had been rather disappointed they weren't going further afield. He'd heard that before the war, Mr Bullock had been to Scotland on business and Daniel longed to travel. He'd wanted to join up to do his bit — and of course, to see more of the world — but he'd been told he was too valuable working in the BTM Company as an engineer because of the sensitive and secret work he was involved in. The team he was part of had developed an amazing new machine for the people at Bletchley Park which they called a Bombe Machine because of the alarming ticking noise it made — just like a real bomb about to go off.

Daniel knew Commander Denniston, the head of Bletchley Park, had often visited Letchworth to discuss the design of the Bombe with BTM's Mr Keen — or Doc, as he was known because of his habit of carrying what looked like a doctor's Gladstone bag. Their first attempt at a machine to decrypt enemy messages had been christened Victory. It was enormous, like a giant metal bookcase containing thirty-six drums which whirred and clicked as they rotated, each simulating the rotor wheels on an Enigma Machine.

The boffins at Bletchley had been delighted with it at first but it hadn't lived up to its promise. It was followed by an improved version which became known as Agnus Dei, or more usually, Aggie. Daniel had only been allowed to carry out minor, insignificant tasks. However he'd soon discovered he understood the electro-mechanical workings and had impressed Doc Keen once by spotting a minor fault in Aggie which had resulted in a persistent short circuit.

'Keep hold of that boy. He shows promise,' Doc Keen had told Mr Bullock within Daniel's hearing. He'd been thrilled, and wrote to his parents that evening, telling them.

He could see his father, sitting by the fire in the kitchen listening as his mother read the letter aloud. Pride would choke her voice and his father would dab milky, myopic eyes, the result of having been gassed in the Great War. He would ask her to read the letter again and they would express their belief in the brilliance of their only son.

There would be no mention of the things they'd given up in order to ensure he received the best education available to the son of a hardware store owner who lived in the impoverished East End of London, because they wouldn't consider the hardship to be of any account. It was enough compensation for all those years of adversity to know Daniel had a proper job and prospects.

Not that he could tell them exactly what he did, because he'd signed the Official Secrets Act — but they knew enough to recognise that all his dedication and hard work had paid off.

Now he was accompanying Mr Bullock on an important trip. He hadn't been his boss's first choice. That honour had fallen to Tony Sinclair who'd been with the company for eight years. But Tony had fallen during the blackout and broken his leg. Mr Bullock had grumbled that he was probably on his way home from the pub. Daniel felt this was likely; Tony often arrived at work with bloodshot eyes, complaining of a headache. The smell of alcohol on his breath was also a clue.

So, Mr Bullock, with much sighing and shaking of his head, informed Daniel he would be going to Bletchley and that he'd better make sure he didn't let the company down.

That wasn't likely. Daniel was determined to do whatever it took to succeed in this job and earn enough to lift his parents out of the hardship they endured because of all they'd done for him.

★ ★ ★

After arriving at Bletchley Station, Mr Bullock booked them into the Swan pub. After leaving their suitcases in their rooms, they walked back to the Bletchley Park estate.

'Leave the talking to me. Is that clear?'

'Yes, sir.'

'I'll need you to take notes, Matthews. And to pay attention.'

'Yes, sir.'

'That may not be as easy as you might think.'

'Sir?'

Mr Bullock scratched his nose.

'Well . . . Bletchley isn't like anywhere else I've ever been. You're going to find it very different.'

'In what way, sir?'

'Well, you could be forgiven for thinking you'd wandered into a place full of mad men. And women . . . Too many blasted women for my liking.'

'Commander Denniston seems quite normal when he comes to Letchworth, sir.'

'Well, yes, he is. But as for the others . . . That Dilly chap's got a dreadful temper and he sulks like a child. Turing rides to work on a bicycle wearing a gas mask, scaring the locals. The last time I visited Bletchley, Tom Kemp offered to take us to Hut One to see our Bombe Machine. Then instead, he led us into the stationery cupboard. You'd never believe they were such a brainy lot.

'Luckily, they're mostly harmless. But when you put so many unusual people together, normal rules seem to go by the by.'

'Normal rules, sir?'

Sensing he hadn't been clear, Mr Bullock continued, 'There are a lot of young people at Bletchley. Many about your age, I'd say. For some, it's the first time they've been away from home. I've heard rumours about them running amok.

'Now, don't get me wrong, lad, I was young once and believe it or not, I understand how a nicely turned pair of female ankles might turn a man's head . . . ' He scratched his nose again and Daniel noticed his colour had heightened. 'But you've got to be on yer guard, see? Women are as slippery as eels and just when you think they're about to wriggle away, you find they've got their fangs in you and it's you that's been caught.'

Daniel swallowed and stared ahead at the pavement. Did Mr Bullock know about Sybil Mills?

'You're a good-looking young fellow, Matthews, and I see the attention you get from the young ladies. So far, I've had no cause to complain.'

He doesn't know! Daniel slowly let out the breath he'd been holding.

'But I can't afford for you to be distracted. There's too much at stake — for the company and for the war effort at Bletchley.'

'No, sir.'

'So, think with your head and not . . . ' he looked sideways at Daniel and allowed his gaze to slide downwards, 'anywhere else, if you get my drift. Give the girls a wide berth. Of course, you won't need to worry about the Debs. Those girls in pearls are way out of your league. You wouldn't get anywhere near them anyway. Their sole aim is to marry well, and any whiff of scandal would put paid to that. But there are plenty of other women working there.'

'I understand, Mr Bullock.' Daniel nodded gravely. He did — and he agreed wholeheartedly. He was quite happy to forgo any feminine company for the foreseeable future.

His stomach lurched as he remembered how close he'd come to risking all he'd worked for, in much the same way as Mr Bullock had described — although his description of wriggling eels suggested slime and coldness. Sybil Mills had guided his hands to all those warm, soft places which he'd been wondering about for the last few years. And she'd touched him in a way which had inflamed his passions so strongly, he'd forgotten all his mother's warnings.

There'd been no room for common sense as Sybil carried him along on a wave of pleasure.

Even her whispered comment that she knew he was a good man and would stand by her if things went wrong, had momentarily puzzled him but hadn't stopped him pulling her closer. The sound of Sybil's mother on the doorstep outside, dropping her keys and cursing loudly, however, had stopped him in much the same way as a dousing with a bucket of cold water might have.

They'd sprung apart and luckily, Mrs Mills had fumbled with the keys, giving her daughter enough time to do up her blouse buttons and run her fingers through her hair. She was waiting calmly in the passage when the door finally opened.

'Get us a cuppa, there's a good girl,' Mrs Mills greeted her. 'My fingers are so cold, I need something to warm 'em up.'

They'd gone into the kitchen and as soon as Daniel had put on his coat, he slipped out of the parlour into the street. The cold wind hit him like a slap in the face, bringing him back to reality. He hadn't expected his evening to turn out like that.

Of course, he'd been flattered when Sybil had asked him to walk her home, saying she thought she'd been followed the previous evening. And he'd truly expected the cup of tea she'd offered.

Not that he was trying to shift the blame to her completely. He could have stopped her when it became clear what her real intentions were, but he hadn't. He'd thrilled at her touch and wanted to explore more — until her mother had unexpectedly returned and he'd come to his senses.

Daniel wasn't sure if eels had fangs but he understood Mr Bullock's analogy. Hadn't his mother warned him against girls like Sybil? Ma had wanted him to make his own decisions, not be limited by someone else's demands — and the comment about him being a good man and standing by her *if things went wrong* had, once he'd thought about it, been remarkably clear.

And hadn't Daniel's best friend, Ronnie, just become a reluctant husband and shortly after, a father? Although Daniel suspected it had been Ronnie who'd pursued his new wife, rather than the other way around.

'Well, let's hope you do see, lad.' Mr Bullock shook his head. 'Yer face is goin' to let you down, I fear. Too handsome for yer own good.'

Daniel blushed. 'I'm very ambitious, sir,' he said in an effort to change the subject.

Mr Bullock sighed deeply.

'I'm not unsympathetic, lad. I was young once meself, although that might be hard for you to believe. And I know what it's like to come from . . . shall we say, the less desirable parts of London. Climbing the social ladder, getting away from our roots, takes determination. People above don't want you to succeed, and people below — for a variety of reasons — will try to pull you back down.

'I know what it takes, lad. I grew up in Bethnal Green, not a million miles from your family home in Stepney. I climbed up that ladder. The question is, will you?'

'I will, Mr Bullock,' Daniel said. He'd been determined before but now, he would redouble his efforts. He hadn't known his boss had been an East End boy, nor that he knew anything about Daniel's background. With a stab of fear, he wondered if Mr Bullock knew about Sybil after all.

It will never happen again, he promised himself.

* * *

Tom looked puzzled. 'Is that the air raid siren?'

'Yes, come on! We've got to get to the shelter . . .

Tom, what are you looking for?' Jess grabbed her handbag and ran to the door.

'Where's my copy of *The Iliad*? If I'm going to be cooped up, I want something to read.'

'It's on the shelf. Come on! Please hurry!'

'But we've never had an air raid at Bletchley before,' Tom said pensively, peering at the shelf.

'Well, we're having one now, Tom!' Jess rushed towards him, grabbed the book and urged him out of the office. She took his arm and, in the courtyard, they joined Gwen and the girls who worked with Dilly Knox, who were already spilling out of the cottages, with arms full of whatever they considered worth saving from a bomb blast.

As they hurried to the shelter Jess saw Louis running in the opposite direction, eyes wide.

'Have you seen Alan? He's gone missing!'

'No, but we had some people coming from the British Tabulating Machine Company today. Perhaps he's with them?' one of Dilly's girls shouted as she passed him.

Jess stopped to wait for Louis who, having satisfied himself Alan wasn't in his office, carried on to Dilly's cottage.

'Come on, Jess!' Gwen called over her shoulder as she moved quickly towards the shelter with the others. Obviously, Alan wasn't there either but instead of joining the crowd, Louis ran off in the other direction.

Jess waited; she didn't want to go until she knew he was safe but as she hesitated, Tom suggested there might be time to go back for another book. Jess insisted he follow the others.

They'd only just made it into the bunker when the first bomb exploded, shaking the ground and raining dust down on them.

'That was close,' Gwen whispered.

'I'm sure we'll be all right, Jess,' Gwen said, putting her arm around her, obviously misreading her horrified expression.

'It's not me I'm worried about. It's Louis. He was looking for Alan earlier and he won't have made it here in time.'

'Most of the huts have anti-bomb blast walls surrounding them. I'm sure he'll have found somewhere to go. He'll be as safe in one of the huts as we are here.'

'That's the first time Bletchley's been bombed since we've been here,' Tom said matter-of-factly as if discussing the day's menu in the canteen.

Another explosion rocked the shelter,

followed by two more which were further away. People coughed in the dust-laden air and several moaned softly. The lights flickered and died, plunging the already gloomy interior of the shelter into utter darkness before those who'd had the forethought to bring torches were able to switch them on and slice through the blackness.

Everyone strained to hear the tell-tale sound of another falling bomb but other than an enormous, ground-shaking thud which strangely, wasn't followed by an explosion, there was nothing. They waited silently, hoping for the all clear, nerves stretched taut.

Shortly after, the siren's continuous tone brought the crowd surging out into the open, looking up to make sure the threat had really gone. A red glow could be seen over the trees.

'Looks like Elmers School's taken a direct hit. Gosh, I hope Gordon Welchman and his team got out in time,' Gwen said, staring in horror at the column of smoke rising into the sky.

Despite the explosions which had seemed so close, the mansion appeared unscathed.

However they were prevented from going back to the stable yard by a sergeant.

'Sorry, ladies, there's an unexploded bomb in the stable yard. You won't be going back there until it's been dealt with. And don't go near Hut Four. One o' them bombs lifted it off its foundations. It'll be a few days before things're back to normal.'

'I've got to find Louis!' Jess craned her neck.

'Well, ye're not goin' that way!' the sergeant said, puffing his chest out. 'We're shifting the casualties. Yer wouldn't want to be obstructive now, would you, ladies?'

'No, sergeant, of course not,' said Gwen soothingly. She took Jess's arm and pulled her after the crowd who were being herded away from the unexploded bomb in the stable yard.

As they made their way to the front of the mansion, Jess scanned faces for

Louis, hoping he wasn't one of the casualties the sergeant had referred to. She consoled herself with the thought there'd been no mention of fatalities — yet.

Her nostrils were filled with the distinctive smell of the aftermath of a bomb raid, so frequent at Holsmere — the brick and plaster dust, smoke, charred timber, the faintest whiff of escaping gas. There had been plenty of deaths then . . .

Panic rose in her. Suppose Louis hadn't made it to a shelter and hadn't yet been found? He could be lying anywhere in the grounds, wounded and bleeding. The thought of Louis being hurt was an almost physical pain and she thought back to nights when friends had paced back and forth, their faces white and strained, waiting to hear whether their sweethearts' Wellington Bombers had landed safely back at Holsmere.

Now she understood. It didn't matter that Louis hadn't displayed more than friendship to her. She knew she loved him and if anything had happened to him, she wouldn't be able to bear it.

Jess had no idea there were so many people on the Bletchley estate. It was as if someone had lifted a rock and suddenly, a swarm of ants could be seen. And this vast number of people was merely one shift, and therefore only represented a third of all the people working on the site. If only she were taller and could see more faces, she thought, standing on tiptoe.

Miss Abernethy was waiting on the mansion entrance steps, briskly waving the girls over.

'Oh, thank goodness!' she said, gripping a clipboard tightly. 'Commander Denniston's supposed to be holding a meeting with these two gentlemen from the British Tabulating Machine Company but I can't find Dilly. You haven't seen him, have you?'

'He was in the shelter with us, so he's safe,' Gwen said.

Miss Abernethy groaned. 'Every time I locate one person, another goes missing. Gordon Welchman and Tom Kemp are already with the commander in his office but I need to take Mr Bullock up there too.' She gestured to the elder of the two men. 'Then I need to find Colonel Tiltman and let him know the meeting is resuming. Then, there's Alan Turing. He's in Hut 1 with Louis Gresham.'

Jess gasped. Louis was safe!

'I've to take Mr Matthews to Hut 1 to talk to Louis and I simply can't be in three places at the same time. Can you help?' Miss Abernethy said.

Jess stepped forward quickly. 'I'll take Mr Matthews to Hut 1,' she said eagerly.

'Thank you, Jess,' Miss Abernethy said, not noticing the older man from the British Tabulating Machine Company frown. 'Don't forget to bring Alan back with you.'

'I don't want to put anyone out. I'm sure I can find my own way,' Mr Matthews said coldly.

'If you don't mind,' said Miss Abernethy, 'I'd rather Jess took you. I'm afraid you won't be allowed in without an escort.'

Mr Matthews nodded politely and

avoided eye contact with Jess. Instead, he looked anxiously at Mr Bullock who pressed his lips together.

'I'll fetch Colonel Tiltman, if you like,' said Gwen.

'Excellent!' said Miss Abernethy, checking her wristwatch, oblivious to the silent interchange between the two guests from the British Tabulating Machine Company.

★ ★ ★

'Is this your first time at Bletchley?' Jess asked the young man whose face was set in a scowl.

'Yes,' he replied in a tone which didn't invite further discussion.

She wondered if he'd been shaken up by the bomb raid. He appeared to be about her age, which was young to have a position of importance at the British Tabulating Machine Company, so perhaps he was nervous among all the university dons, especially if it was his first time on the site.

'I haven't been here long,' Jess said, trying to put him at his ease. 'How long have you been in your current job?'

'I thought no one was supposed to talk about what they do at Bletchley?'

'I . . . I was only making conversation,' Jess said. 'And I didn't talk about what I did.'

The young man simply stared ahead in silence.

How rude, Jess thought. *What a thoroughly unpleasant man.*

They entered Hut 1 and to Jess's delight, Louis's face lit up when he saw them. He strode towards them, hand outstretched and shook the man's hand.

'Mr Matthews! How good to see you again! And such superb timing. Alan and I were just sorting this mess out.' Louis led him over to Alan, who was peering at a bundle of wires which resembled tangled knitting wool.

Jess's delight drained away, leaving bitter disappointment. She'd mistaken Louis's pleasure at seeing the rude man, believing it was relief that she was well after the bombing raid, but he'd barely acknowledged her presence.

We're at war, she told herself, *of course Louis would be focused on his work.* Cracking the enemy codes was paramount. Usually, he was a thoughtful and kind man who wouldn't have deliberately ignored her. There were bigger things at stake here than her feelings.

She was about to leave when she remembered Miss Abernethy had sent her to make sure Alan Turing attended the meeting. Fixing a smile on her face, she approached the three men who were animatedly discussing a problem with one of the rotating drums which Alan was holding up for the other two men.

How alive Louis looked. How utterly absorbed.

Jess didn't want to interrupt, but Miss Abernethy had stressed that Alan was needed . . .

'Excuse me please,' she said nervously, cutting into their conversation.

The three men looked at her with irritation.

'Miss Abernethy asked me to ensure Alan goes to the meeting with Commander Denniston.'

Alan looked at his wristwatch.

'Yes, yes, I just need to explain this to Mr Matthews and I'll be right with you,' he said pointing to the drum standing on his palm.

Jess backed away to the door.

'Crikey! You've got all the luck!' one of the Wrens who was operating the Bombe Machine whispered to her. 'What a heart-throb! When you've finished with him, let me know!' She winked at Jess. 'What's his name?'

'Louis Gresham,' Jess said, taken aback at the Wren's attempts to catch his eye.

'Not Louis! I know him all right! He's always in here tinkering with the machines.' She fluttered her eyelashes at the men, laughing when she caught Mr Matthews' eye and he turned his face away. 'Him, the new bloke, he's the one I mean!'

'Matthews. I don't know his first name

though.'

'You haven't found out the name of a man who looks like a cross between Clark Gable, Robert Taylor and Errol Flynn? Crikey, love, take your glasses off and give them a good clean!'

'He looks nothing like those actors,' said Jess crossly. 'Anyway, they're all dark, he's blond!'

It wasn't until Mr Matthews glared at her and turned away that she realised she'd not only raised her voice but was pointing at him.

'Well, I think he's a darling.' The Wren laughed and blew him a kiss.

Finally, Alan finished his conversation and followed Jess back to the mansion.

* * *

'You seem glum tonight, Jessica,' Phyllis said. Why did she find it so hard to hide her feelings?

Her face always betrayed her innermost thoughts.

The girls had just returned from work

and were eating supper together. It had been a week since the bombing raid and Jess had hardly seen Louis at work. The men from the British Tabulating Machine Company were still at Bletchley and Louis had been with them most of the time.

Jess had joined the Scottish Dancing Society and the Chess Club at Louis's suggestion several weeks before — but since Mr Bullock and Mr Matthews had arrived, Louis hadn't had time to attend.

'Man trouble,' said Gwen. 'Don't deny it, Jess. I have a sixth sense for affairs of the heart.'

'Do tell!' said Phyllis.

'Oh, it's nothing,' said Jess, hoping they'd lose interest.

'It can't be nothing,' said Edna with a hint of irritation in her voice. 'You've been moping about for days now.'

'Well, it's just that I rather like some-one and he doesn't seem to know I exist.'

'Hmm,' said Phyllis, 'that's a tricky problem. So, Gwen, you're the expert in all matters romantic. What do you sug-gest?'

155

'I didn't say I'm an expert! I could just tell Jess was pining for someone. My experience is pretty limited. Peter's away in the Middle East and I haven't seen him for ages. Things were so new between us before he went away, I'm not really sure how I feel about him now anyway.'

'Gracious! You're not thinking of breaking things off with him, are you?'

'No,' Gwen said slowly. 'I'll wait until he comes home on leave and then see. But I'm often too busy to write and his letters are getting less and less frequent. I wouldn't be surprised if he hasn't found a nurse or someone and wants to finish with me.'

'Oh, Gwen, I'm so sorry,' said Phyllis.

'It's fine, really. I'm not upset or anything. I didn't see us settling down together or anything — despite my parents steering me in that direction. In fact, I'm quite enjoying myself being single and not having to worry about making a good match.'

'Me too,' said Phyllis with a sigh. 'This war's changing everything. A few years ago, I imagined I'd meet someone during my first Season after I'd come out into society. Now, well, I don't know.'

'What nonsense you both talk!' said Edna. 'It's our birthright! I want to get married!'

'Well, no one's stopping you,' said Gwen. 'But I'm thinking of getting a job after the war's over and living my life as I want.'

'You'll end up old and on your own,' warned Edna darkly.

'And you might end up old and living with someone you can't stand!'

'What about you, Jessica? What are your thoughts for the future?' Phyllis asked, before Edna and Gwen could carry on their argument.

'I . . . suppose I always thought I'd get married like my parents, but . . . ' She tailed off sadly.

'I expect your parents have some young farmer or the like in mind for you, Jess,' Edna said.

'Sometimes, Edna, you can be so patronising!' Gwen exclaimed.

'Actually, they won't have given me a thought since I left the vicarage. As for marriage, well, no one ever mentioned it. So long as I don't live a life of loose morals, I don't expect they care.'

There was silence after Jess's reply. Gwen placed an arm around her and glared at Edna who, for once, didn't come back with a retort.

'That can't be right, Jessica,' Phyllis said. 'They must care, surely?'

Jess bit her bottom lip and shook her head.

'Then it's entirely up to you to choose what you want to do,' said Gwen firmly. 'And at least you won't have any parental interference to worry about.'

'Easier said than done,' said Jess despondently. 'I've never really liked a man before . . . and now I've fallen for one, he doesn't seem to like me.'

'Doesn't like you or hasn't noticed you?' Phyllis asked. 'There is a difference, you know.'

'We get on well, but just as friends.'

'So, we need to work on a strategy for

him to notice you and realise he can't live without you.'

'I . . . don't think I could do anything too daring . . .'

'Nonsense,' declared Gwen. 'You need to be brought out of yourself.'

'You can't make a silk purse out of a sow's ear,' said Edna.

'Thank you for your thoughts, Edna. But in future, why don't you bally well keep them to yourself?' Phyllis said tartly. 'Jessica needs to have her confidence built up. Not flattened.'

'Why can't any of you take a joke?' Edna said sulkily.

'It's strange how your jokes always sound so serious — and so nasty!' Gwen fired back.

'Do stop your bickering!' Phyllis commanded. 'We need a way to help Jessica boost her confidence.'

'You need to reinvent yourself, Jess,' said Gwen. 'And I've got the perfect idea. Join the Drama Society with Phyllis and me.'

Jess blanched. 'Oh, I . . . I'm not

sure . . . '

'Oh, don't worry, the parts for the Christmas Revue have already been cast for this year. You'll just be put in the chorus. Do say you'll join us, Jess.'

* * *

There was nothing immoral about making yourself the centre of attention. Jess knew that — despite her father's many warnings to convince her otherwise.

And yet . . . the thought of so many people staring at her . . . even if she was only a member of the chorus.

She turned over and pulled the bed covers up to her chin, desperate for sleep. Her eyes ached and her forehead was tight. It had been a long day poring over pages covered in sets of five letters.

It had been a day like any other.

The initial excitement of discovering what went on at Bletchley had given way to the mind-numbing acceptance that her work was monotonous and unrelenting. Albeit vital.

Tom, after his initial diffidence, had come to value her input and to rely on her to organise his office and his life, and she was beginning to think of him as an elder brother. And Louis brought excitement into her life whenever he came into the office. But other than that, her working day was long and tedious.

And now, she was angry with herself for once again being influenced by her father and his outdated opinions. She'd already decided to join the Dramatic Society — if only to prove to herself that her father no longer had any hold over her. But every time she closed her eyes, she began to imagine herself on a stage, spotlights dazzling her and an audience staring.

She suspected there would in fact be no spotlights. This was under-resourced Bletchley Park, not a London theatre. It would be an amateur show; no one would expect a polished performance.

Perhaps she could hide at the back of the chorus. Yes, that was it. She was so short, she could disappear into the crowd. Or, even better, volunteer to make costumes or do make-up. Sweep up, even.

And, she told herself, Louis had a part in the revue and he wouldn't be allowed to miss rehearsals so close to Christmas — even if the men from the British Tabulating Machine Company were there. She could build up her confidence and spend time with Louis as well.

Finally, she drifted off to sleep.

* * *

Jess was right about Louis attending rehearsals and his face lit up the following evening when he saw her with Phyllis and Gwen.

'You didn't tell me you were coming! But that's wonderful. Several people have had to drop out.'

'Come and meet the director,' said Phyllis, taking her arm and leading her towards a tall man with a mane of thick, white hair. 'He's directed several West End plays, you know,' she added.

162

A pink and green Paisley cravat at his throat stood out against the director's black suit and he waved a matching handkerchief with an elegant hand as he instructed people where to stand.

'Julian B. Frobisher, pleased to meet you,' he said, nodding at Jess as Phyllis introduced her. The glasses resting on the top of his head swung forward and landed on his nose. He pushed them into place and with his handkerchief, waved her towards the raised area which was obviously the stage. 'Join the chorus, there's a dear.'

Jess had been wrong. There were spotlights. The performance was going to take place in the hall in the mansion but still, someone had managed to acquire some large lights which were temporarily rigged up at ceiling height. But there was still quite a crowd standing on one side of the stage and Jess was sure she could slip behind and disappear from sight.

However, she'd underestimated Mr Frobisher's powers of observation.

'New girl! Stand at the front, please!' he shouted as Jess tried to slip behind the group. Reluctantly, she made her way to the front.

'No! No! No!' Mr Frobisher yelled and Jess jumped, assuming she'd done something wrong. But his attention was now on the man next to him who'd handed him a message.

'This is impossible!' he raged, his booming voice reaching all corners of the hall. Sliding his spectacles to the top of his head, he mopped his brow with his handkerchief. Everyone paused and watched to find out what had happened.

'Ladies and gentlemen,' Mr Frobisher declaimed. 'I'm afraid Mr Bancroft's hand is now infected and it's unlikely he'll be able to play the piano for our revue.'

People groaned.

'He cut his hand on broken glass when the bomb went off,' the man next to Jess whispered.

'Is there anyone who could take his place?' Mr Frobisher boomed, turning on his heel so as to survey everyone in the hall.

A girl stepped out of the chorus and hesitantly held up her hand. 'Admirable, Miss Austin, truly admirable,' said Mr Frobisher, 'but I'm afraid you're far too valuable in the chorus and I'm going to have to insist you remain there.'

'Thank goodness for that!' the man next to Jess whispered, 'She played at the last rehearsal and she's tone deaf.'

'Is there anyone else? Please?' Mr Frobisher said.

'Ken Horsnall plays,' someone shouted out.

'He's gone down with 'flu,' someone else replied.

'What about Mary Tufnell? She can play. And so can Caroline Yaxley.'

'I need someone now!' Mr Frobisher said waving his handkerchief in frustration.

There was silence for a few seconds, then Louis called out from the other side of the stage.

'Jess can play.'

'Who? Who?' Mr Frobisher said, looking around to locate who'd spoken and then following the direction of Louis's pointing finger, 'Oh, you mean the new girl?'

Jess was so shocked, her protest came out as a squeak. Involuntarily she stepped backwards.

'Come on! Come on! We're already behind.' He beckoned a white-faced Jess and handed her the music as she crept past him on her way to the piano. For a second, she wondered whether she could run away but there were too many people between her and the doors.

She sat down at the piano, drew a deep breath and started to play.

'Stop! Stop!' Mr Frobisher shouted. He rushed over to her. 'Wrong piece. Sorry, I need you to start here.' He stabbed at the music with his finger. 'Don't worry, dear! At least you can play, which is more than Miss Austin can,' he whispered. He turned and cleared his throat. 'Everyone ready now? Let's go from the top . . . '

166

★ ★ ★

The Christmas Revue was a great success. When Jess wasn't working, she practised all the pieces she had to play for the performance and had thrilled when she saw the programmes with her name printed — Pianist — Jessica Langley.

Her initial annoyance with Louis had subsided. After all, he'd had faith in her despite never actually hearing her play. And since Mr Bullock and Mr Matthews had gone back to Letchworth, she'd spent more time with Louis, both at work and at the various clubs they shared.

Jess could hardly wait for Christmas. Phyllis, Gwen and Edna were all going home on leave for a few days but she'd volunteered to stay at Bletchley and work. So had Louis.

'My parents don't really approve of me,' he'd said when she'd asked why he'd volunteered to stay. His explanation was disappointing. She'd held her breath, hoping he'd say it was to be with her over the festive season, but at least she understood.

'Mine neither,' she said.

'Well, more fool all of them! I bet we have a better time here than we would at home!'

A week before Christmas, Jess took a day's leave and travelled to London on the train to look for a present for Louis. She headed towards Oxford Street and spent several hours in Selfridges looking for the perfect gift. Eventually, she bought him a fountain pen. It cost slightly more than she'd wanted to pay but it would be worth it because she knew he'd love it, and she could save money by not eating lunch. That would give her time to walk to Regent Street.

She would merely look, she told herself, just out of curiosity, for the shop which sold undergarments of German parachute silk. But once she'd found it, she had enough for a pair of silk knickers and couldn't resist buying them.

On the way back to Bletchley on the train, she dipped her hand into her bag to stroke the silky fabric and found herself blushing.

'I know, love,' the large woman sitting next to Jess said sympathetically, 'it's bloomin' stuffy in here. I'm 'avin' an 'ot flush too.'

Jess pulled her hand out of her bag guiltily and held the top together tightly, as if she were afraid the silky garment might escape.

* * *

'What d'you think?' Louis said, pulling a pipe tobacco pouch out of a bag, after glancing out of the window to make sure no one was about to enter the office.

'Who's it for?' Jess asked.

'It's Alan's Christmas present.'

'Very nice. I'm sure he'll love it,' Jess said, hoping Louis would like her gift.

'I'll give it to him after Christmas dinner,' Louis said, putting it back inside the bag. 'Don't forget, we'll be doing Scottish dancing in the hall after.'

Jess smiled, assuring him she wouldn't

forget. How could she? She couldn't wait for the day.

Her mother's letter had been brief and formal. She wasn't happy about her daughter not coming home for Christmas although she stopped short of complaining.

Jess hadn't told her she'd volunteered to stay. Rather, she'd suggested she'd been rostered on over Christmas.

However in the same post as her mother's letter was one from William, her brother. He'd been given leave and would be in London shortly after Christmas, and if Jess was free, would she like to meet up? He gave her several dates and asked her to choose one and a place to go.

When she asked Phyllis and Gwen for ideas on where to meet, she expected they'd say Trafalgar Square or somewhere similar but they'd both immediately said, 'Claridge's.'

'I'm not sure where that is,' Jess said.

'Then we'd best remedy that as soon as we've all got leave,' Phyllis said.

Jess wrote back immediately suggesting a date to meet at Claridge's and hoped William would get her letter in time.

* * *

Jess awoke on Christmas morning with a feeling of excitement she'd never before experienced. At St Margaret's Vicarage, it had been viewed as a religious day with minimal fuss. There had been a tree and a large family meal, but it had been stressed that they were merely incidental to the important part of the day — the church service.

This year, Jess would be at work. At lunchtime, she would join Louis for the meal and afterwards, she'd give him his present. Then, there'd be Scottish reels and games until . . . well, she didn't know how long they'd go on for but since Phyllis, Gwen and Edna had already gone home, there would be no car to transport her back to Lestcombe Hall. She would cycle home. And as Louis's billet wasn't far away and as he was a gentleman, he wouldn't leave her at the crossroads — he'd carry on and escort her back to the house.

And then . . .

That was when she was going to tell him how she felt about him. The thought made her weak with fear but she'd discussed her problem with Gwen, who'd said that sometimes men needed a helping hand to be able to express their feelings.

Jess wasn't sure. Louis seemed very confident and forthright. But perhaps Gwen was right. After all, she had a sweetheart whereas Jess had never had one. True, Gwen's fellow had been overseas for months — but she must have more idea about love than Jess.

Louis must have feelings for her. Hadn't he told her things he'd said he hadn't told anyone else? Didn't he seek out her company and spend lots of time with her?

Yes, Gwen must be right; men often needed a gentle nudge. And Christmas

Night would be the time Louis received one.

* * *

There were two reasons why Jess was feeling rather shameful. Firstly, she'd avoided the church service. Not because she had anything against the Christmas morning service — in fact, she would have enjoyed it. It was because it was yet another opportunity to break with all the traditions and values her father had tried to instil in her.

She had, instead, gone straight to work and had been touched when Tom had given her a second-hand copy of a book of odes by Horace, in Latin. She certainly hadn't expected him to think of buying her anything, and had been glad she'd bought him a small gift of a paperweight. He'd been delighted, which touched her. She wouldn't have found it at all surprising if Christmas had come and gone without him noticing.

The second reason was far more

wicked than her deliberate avoidance of the church service. Beneath the smart dress, one that no longer fitted Phyllis and which Mrs Jenner had altered, Jess wore the silk underwear — and every movement felt lusciously decadent.

'I'll translate the odes for you,' Tom said. 'Jess? Jess? Are you listening?'

'Yes, yes, sorry, Tom! That would be lovely.' She looked down at the book he was holding out to her, thinking of how the silk slipped over her skin and wondering if Louis would find it exciting.

When Jess went to see if Louis was ready for lunch, she saw Alan's new tobacco pouch lying on his desk.

'Did he like it?' she asked.

Louis nodded enthusiastically.

It was too early for lunch and Jess thought she might give Louis his present while they were alone, rather than waiting until later. When she held it out, he reddened and laughed nervously.

'A present? For me?' He took the package and swallowed. 'Jess, that's really generous. But . . . I'm really sorry . . .

I don't have anything for you.'

'That's all right. Christmas is about giving.'

'Well, yes, but I feel terrible . . . I wish I'd known . . . I'd have got you something.'

His embarrassment was infectious and she turned away before he unwrapped it, knowing it would be obvious to him that it had been expensive. Perhaps she shouldn't have bought him anything?

Alan poked his head around the door into the office. 'Come on, you two. Don't dawdle. We're all having drinks in Dilly's office before lunch.'

Louis slipped the unwrapped box into his drawer and, leaping to his feet, he smiled at her apologetically, then followed Alan.

* * *

Jess accepted a sherry. It was, after all, Christmas and she suspected there wouldn't be much work done that afternoon. Surely the Germans would be celebrating too, and not sending the usual numbers of messages?

Everyone was in a party mood and it was some time before Alan checked his wristwatch and announced they'd better go or they'd miss lunch. In the crush to get out of the office, Jess found herself at the back of the group.

When they arrived at the dining hall, she was amazed to see the magnificent decorations and the large number of people already seated at the tables.

Dilly's party spread out, taking seats where they could and Jess found herself between two men she knew from the Drama Group. She was disappointed, having imagined a smaller, more intimate meal where she'd be seated next to Louis. He, however, had managed to find a seat further along the table with Alan on one side and Mavis Lever, one of Dilly's Fillies, on the other.

The tables were covered with Christmas fare — turkey, goose, chicken, pies. Jess had never seen such a meal, which was all the more remarkable because of the wartime food shortages.

There was no point being disappointed at not being near Louis, she told herself. He'd invited her to the Scottish dancing later, so there'd still be time to be with him. And Charlie and Arthur, the two men from the Drama Group, were vying for her attention, teasing each other mercilessly.

Each person had a menu and at the end of the meal, someone suggested all the guests should sign each one so that the following Christmas when the war would surely be over, they would all remember who'd been there at Christmas 1940.

How different this day of festivities was to all the others she'd spent at St Margaret's!

Jess knew she'd drunk too much but somehow, rather than affecting her balance and sapping her energy, it seemed to do the opposite, making everything seem more vivid and enjoyable.

Hours later, after the Scottish dancing, those who still remained put on their coats and assembled on the lawn in front of the mansion, their feet crunching on the frosty grass and their breath hanging in clouds as they sang Christmas carols and finished with a rousing and rather drunken *God Save The King*.

Now I'll have him to myself, Jess thought as the group of revellers finally broke up and she and Louis wheeled their bicycles to the entrance.

She was less steady now, but managed to keep on her saddle despite weaving across the road. Louis was in the same state and their progress was slow, as each wobble was met with gales of laughter. But at the crossroads where he should have turned left, he insisted he carry on with her to Lestcombe Hall.

She had known he would. He was, after all, a gentleman and would not allow her to cycle up the shadowy lane on her own.

The hall was dark because of the black-out precautions but music and laughter drifted from the ballroom where Aunt Beatrice's Christmas celebration was still in full swing. Jess and Louis dismounted and pushed their bicycles up the drive, then round the back to the kitchen.

At the door, Louis turned his bicycle, overbalanced and burst out laughing when he almost fell on top of it.

'If I end up in a ditch tonight, it's your fault!' he said and wagged his finger theatrically.

'I can make you coffee if you like,' Jess said, suddenly sobering up. This was the moment she'd been waiting for all day.

'I don't know,' he said uncertainly.

'Please. There's something I want to tell you.'

'That sounds serious!' He leaned his bicycle against the wall and as he turned, she moved in front of him and put her arms around his neck.

'Jess! What are you doing?' He stepped back in alarm and found himself against the wall.

'Louis, I wanted to tell you —'

'Jess, stop it!' He reached behind his neck and pulled her hands away.

'But, Louis, you must know how I feel . . . '

'Stop it, Jess. I'm sorry . . . ' He pushed her gently away.

She gasped and began to sob.

'Jess, please don't. Don't cry.'

'But I love you, Louis! I thought . . . '

'We're friends, Jess,' he said firmly.

She stared at him in silence. Finally, she asked in a small voice, 'What's wrong with me, Louis?'

'Nothing, Jess. You're wonderful — but I thought you knew I had feelings for someone else.'

'Someone else? You never said! You never mentioned anyone!'

'That's because my feelings aren't returned.'

'Then why can't we . . . '

'You really don't know, do you?' he said, his voice choked with emotion.

'All I know is that I love you! If you can't have the one you want, please give me a chance.'

'Jess,' he said firmly, 'I can't.'

'So, who is it you love?'

'Jess, please understand . . . It . . . It's Alan.'

'But. . . How can that be?'

'Oh, darling Jess. I thought you'd guessed. I thought you knew. Please don't hate me. I really like you. I really value your friendship. And I truly wish I could be what you want me to be . . . but I can't.'

He took the handlebars of the bicycle and wheeled it away without looking back.

5

'Jess!' Gwen said, her face frozen in shock. 'I had no idea it was Louis Gresham you were keen on! Oh, my dear, if only I'd known!'

'What's wrong with Louis Gresham?' Edna asked. 'He seems like a nice young man.'

'Yes,' said Phyllis. 'What's wrong with him?'

Gwen sighed. 'Nothing wrong exactly . . . unless of course you've got feelings for him, like Jess.'

'I still don't see,' said Edna.

'He prefers the company of men,' Gwen said firmly.

'Well, lots of men prefer . . . ' Edna paused. 'Oh, I see! You mean he prefers as in . . . *prefers*?'

'I didn't know Louis preferred men,' said Phyllis, putting her arm around Jess's shoulders, 'but then I don't really see that much of him at work. How do you know, Gwen?'

'Well, I wasn't absolutely sure because Louis is not obvious about it like Alan Turing — '

'Alan Turing?' Edna said, her voice raised in surprise. 'You mean to tell me *he* prefers men?'

'Even I knew that,' said Phyllis, 'but then Alan's quite open about his preferences.'

'Well, it doesn't matter who knew what. We're not helping Jess at all.'

'I feel so stupid,' Jess wailed. 'There were so many clues but I just didn't notice.'

Looking back, it was obvious. Louis's face lighting up whenever Alan came into the office, the expensive tobacco pouch, the enthusiasm with which he spoke about Alan's achievements and brilliance. But Jess had taken them all at face value, seeing someone who had admiration for his boss rather than someone who was in love.

She'd been shocked when she'd realised Alan was homosexual. He'd been quite open about it, which had helped Jess to come to terms with it.

In the past, her father had vehemently condemned homosexuality from the pulpit, quoting verses from the Bible to reinforce his damning indictment. But then, it had been so far out of her experience as to be irrelevant — her childish imagination, only capable of conjuring up men from Sodom and Gomorrah dressed in Old Testament robes. Exactly what such men did to draw down her father's contempt and anger had been a mystery and she instinctively knew it would be unwise to ask.

Since she'd been at Bletchley, Alan Turing had been kind to her and it had been hard to reconcile her experience of him with the iniquity her father had described. Her rush to reject all Rev Langley's values had made it easier to conclude that whoever Alan was attracted to, was none of her business. She'd had no idea that he would feature prominently in her heartbreak — although to be fair to Alan, he wasn't interested in

Louis. He'd been spending a lot of time with Joan Clarke who worked in Hut 8 and some people suggested that, as unlikely as it seemed, they were romantically linked. If that was so, why couldn't Louis give her a chance too?

'Jess? Jess?' It was Gwen. 'We're going to take your mind off things. How about a night out in London next week?'

'I've got one day's leave next week and I'm meeting my brother in the evening,' Jess said, putting a brave smile on her face to convince the three girls who were peering at her sympathetically that she was all right.

'Actually,' said Phyllis, 'I'm not sure I'll be able to get leave next week.'

'Me neither,' said Edna.

'It's just you and me, then, Jess,' Gwen declared. 'I know! We'll go to London early and I'll take you for afternoon tea in Claridge's, then you'll be there ready to meet your brother.'

'Thank you,' Jess said. She was close to tears at Gwen's thoughtfulness.

'You know . . . there's much to be

said for families arranging matches for their children,' said Edna reflectively. 'At least then both parties go into a relationship with their eyes open.'

'And what about romance?' Gwen asked.

'It's overrated, if you ask me.' Edna sniffed.

★ ★ ★

Louis kept away from Tom's office — and from Jess. Alan and Dilly had gone to London to meet with French cryptanalysts and Louis remained alone in his office. Whenever he emerged, he hurried across the stable yard, head lowered.

One morning Jess arrived at work to find a parcel on her desk with her name written on the paper. The accompanying card read, *To Jess, Sorry for not being what you need. I admired this on you at the ball and it seems appropriate. My warmest regards, Louis G.*

She unwrapped the parcel to find a bottle of Schiaparelli's Shocking perfume.

Did he really believe he could make everything better with a gift? She was tempted to drop it in the bin but Shocking, she knew, was expensive. It was almost certainly more than Louis would have been able to afford. Yet he'd bought it for her to . . . to what? Apologise? Compensate for his lack of affection? Well, at least he cared enough to try.

'You look unhappy, Jess,' Tom said, making her jump. She'd thought he'd been engrossed in his work but he was surveying her over steepled fingers. For once, his attention was all on her.

'I'm fine, thanks.' She fixed on a smile.

He raised his eyebrows in disbelief and stood up. 'It's at times like these I find poetry helps.' He took a battered book off the shelf and dragged his chair across to her desk.

Jess was touched. She'd seen Tom as a brilliant man with great intellectual powers who lacked emotional depth. But that wasn't true. He read out a poem to her with great feeling and then translated it from the Latin with equal passion.

'Good afternoon, madam,' the head hall porter said as Gwen led Jess into the Art Deco splendour of Claridge's lobby. 'I trust the Honourable Misses Briggs and Houghton are well?'

'Yes, thank you, Connors. May I introduce my friend, Miss Jessica Langley.'

'Pleased to meet you, Miss,' Connors said. 'By the way, madam, Lord Byforth's back. And it's a pity you missed Captain Reynolds last week.'

'Captain Reynolds?'

'Yes, madam. I thought it odd you didn't meet him.'

'Unfortunately I couldn't get leave,' Gwen said, her cheeks reddening.

'Is Captain Reynolds your sweetheart?' Jess whispered as they walked towards the Foyer where Gwen had booked afternoon tea.

'I'm not sure now,' Gwen said with a frown. 'He didn't say he was going to be in London.'

'But how did the porter know?'

'Connors knows where everyone is — who's on leave, who's not and where they're staying while they're in London. He seems to make it his business to know everyone else's business and he's got a phenomenal memory. If he says Peter was here last week, he was. I assume that if he didn't bother to contact me, he hasn't got the nerve to tell me it's over.'

'Oh, Gwen, I'm so sorry.'

'Strangely, I'm not,' said Gwen. 'After we've had tea, I'm going to telephone a few people and see if I can find out more. When you've finished with William, we can travel home together.'

* * *

'Well, look at you!' William said, holding Jess at arm's length, 'My little mouse has grown up!'

'I'd hoped you'd forgotten that nickname,' she said and playfully slapped his arm.

Over dinner he told her about Alexandria, where he'd been posted. She told

189

him she was doing clerical work.

'You gave up work on an RAF station to file paper?' he asked in disbelief and Jess changed the subject before he could press her further.

'Have you been home?' she asked.

He shook his head. 'No. I can't see me going home in the foreseeable future. I expect they moaned about my lack of gratitude all Christmas.'

'Probably,' said Jess. 'And mine too, I expect. I didn't go home either.'

'Well, good for you!' William said with feeling. 'They treated you abominably.' He paused and ran a finger around the rim of his wine glass. 'In fact, that was one reason I wanted to see you . . . I've felt very guilty about walking out and leaving you. But I was so young when I left, I don't suppose anyone would've taken any notice of me. Father always believes he's right and Mother always takes his side. But they were both wrong to blame you for Clara's death.'

'They never actually said,' Jess said in alarm.

190

'They didn't have to, Jess — they made it obvious in everything they did.'

'Oh, if only I hadn't pushed Clara into playing hide and seek . . . '

'No one pushed Clara into anything she didn't want to do. If she hadn't wanted to play, she wouldn't have. And we'd all been forbidden to go down to the river without an adult. Clara chose to go there. No. It was a tragic accident but it wasn't your fault. I think it was easier for them to pretend it was. Easier than shouldering the blame themselves. But they were the adults. They should have protected us . . . Anyway, I'm glad you've broken away from them now.'

Brother and sister smiled at each other.

'I know we didn't have much to do with each other when we were growing up but now, I feel very close to you,' William said. 'From now on, I'll always be there for you.' He poured her another glass of wine and they clinked glasses. 'To the future,' he said and they both knew they were making a pact to forget past regrets.

Gwen was waiting in the bar as the girls had arranged, and William stayed to chat to her while Jess went to the ladies' room. When she returned, she was surprised to see her brother flirting with Gwen who was responding. Jess wondered if he knew Gwen was Lady Gwendoline Armstrong-Court. Would it bother him? Probably not. But it would most likely be an issue for Gwen. It was one thing taking a vicar's daughter under your wing to be charitable, but quite another starting a romance with someone of a lower class.

Still, she told herself, they were merely flirting.

Two days later, three letters arrived at Lestcombe Hall. One was to Gwen from Captain Peter Reynolds apologising for not having contacted her when he was on leave and informing her he'd met someone else. The other two were from William — one for Jess and one for Gwen.

6

Daniel was waved off by his parents at the railway station. He'd spent Christmas with them, but now he had to return to his digs in Letchworth to resume work.

As people were still enjoying the relative quiet of the season, the Luftwaffe had struck in an attack more ferocious than any during the previous weeks of the London Blitz.

On December the twenty-ninth, a bomb had dropped in their street, causing enormous damage to the Matthews' home and adjacent houses. They had stayed in a school overnight and then Daniel's parents accepted an invitation to stay with Mrs Matthews' sister in Essex.

The bomb was one of more than 100,000 dropped that night by the Luftwaffe on the capital, resulting in what had been dubbed 'The Second Great Fire of London' by an American journalist. For three and a half hours, incendiary bombs and high-explosive devices rained down on the capital, causing fires to rage from St Paul's Cathedral to Islington, killing over one hundred civilians and firemen, and injuring many more.

Two days later, a photograph published in the Daily Mail showed St Paul's Cathedral, apparently undamaged, surrounded by raging fires and billowing smoke, standing proudly, displaying defiance at anything Hitler could throw at it. The image had given heart to the nation.

Nevertheless, the damage had been immense. The dust and smoke had affected Mr Matthews' lungs, already burned by gas during the Great War, and he fought for breath, his voice weak and rasping. As they said goodbye at the station, he had clasped his son's hand tightly, his milky eyes filled with tears.

Mrs Matthews clasped her son tightly to her and whispered, 'Be safe, son.' Her lip trembled as she let him go and took her husband's arm.

His mother and father looked back

at him as if by a pre-arranged signal. Both turning towards each other, then over their linked arms, back at their son. He waved. They were soon lost from sight among the crowds of servicemen and women and other passengers. But he could still picture their faces — eyes glowing brightly with pride for their son, yet full of fear for the future.

Unbidden, the face of Sybil Mills slipped into his mind, her lips parted and eyes full of promise. He shivered. It wasn't fair. She'd been the instigator. He'd have been quite happy to have walked her home and then to have continued on to his flat. Gratitude for being chivalrous hadn't been on his mind. Nor had her soft, inviting body.

Why, he wondered, over and over, should he feel guilty? He'd walked into the situation blind.

But deep down he was ashamed because he recognised he'd passed a tipping point. After the initial shock, he'd been a willing participant. There'd been no thoughts of his parents nor of doing the right thing — no thoughts at all. Just a sensation that eclipsed everything in its intensity.

He felt ashamed. His thoughts should be on his displaced parents, on their way to his aunt's.

He would not think of Sybil again, and he would not place himself in such a position where he seemed to have no will-power. Work was the only thing that totally absorbed his mind and thankfully, he would return to Letchworth in the morning. Mr Bullock was very pleased with him and now favoured him over feckless Tony Sinclair. His life was back on track, and he was more determined than ever to provide a better life for his parents.

★ ★ ★

'Bletchley Park?' Daniel said in surprise.

'Yes, Matthews. The people we're making Bombe Machines for. Have you forgotten?' Mr Bullock rolled his eyes. 'Perhaps you'd rather I took Tony . . . ?'

'Oh no, sir! I just hadn't expected to

go again so soon.'

'Well, get used to it, Matthews. You and I will probably be back and forth to there for the duration of the war.'

'Yes, sir.'

Daniel smiled. Mr Bullock now treated him as his assistant, no longer even considering Tony Sinclair, who made it clear to Daniel he was looking for an opportunity to discredit him and regain favour.

'Watch yer back, Matthews!' he'd said with a sneer when he'd returned to work after his leg had healed and he realised he'd been replaced in their boss's favour and estimation.

Daniel wasn't unduly worried. He worked hard, kept out of trouble and luckily enjoyed good health so unlike Tony, he took little time off sick.

At least being at Bletchley Park meant time away from the unpleasant scowl of Tony. With so many brilliant minds and imaginations working together — and sometimes working against each other — the requests and suggestions from the boffins were always surprising and inspiring.

Daniel had been to Bletchley several times with Mr Bullock and each time, his head had buzzed with ideas by the time he left. Once back in Letchworth, they'd spent hours in Doc's office discussing possible modifications to the Bombe Machines. Daniel knew both Doc and Mr Bullock were impressed with his suggestions and enthusiasm and he wondered how much longer he'd have to wait for promotion.

Surely not long. That would be something that would brighten his parents' lives and ease him up the ladder towards a better future.

On their arrival at the Park, Daniel was pleased to see Louis Gresham and to know they'd be working together again. The last time Daniel had gone to Hut 1 on his own, one of the Wrens had made it clear she wanted to get to know him. She'd flirted outrageously and had only stopped when her senior officer had overheard her and had threatened to put her on a charge if she didn't get back to work. The girl's name was Sally and she'd tucked a scrap of paper with her address on it into his coat pocket when no one was looking. He'd thrown it away without even glancing at it, and had no intention of following up on her invitations. She didn't appeal to him at all. He preferred tall, willowy, blondes, like Sybil. Sally was small and dark — although they were both too forward and demanding for his liking.

Daniel had noticed that when Louis was there, Sally didn't pester him. Perhaps it was because he was Alan Turing's assistant or perhaps it was because Sally didn't want an audience — but whatever the reason, it would make things easier with Louis there working alongside him.

This time, the usually cheerful Louis was distracted and silent but at least when they were in Hut 1, none of the Wrens bothered them.

It was beginning to get dark but there was enough light for Louis to show Daniel the half-built concrete, blast-proof hut which would house the new Bombe

Machines they'd ordered from the BTM Company.

Hut 11, as the new building was to be called, would be finished by March ready for the delivery of new Bombe Machines. But even the prospect of the completed hut and new machines didn't seem to enthuse the usually exuberant Louis.

Daniel didn't know him well enough to ask if anything was wrong and there probably wouldn't be much he could do about it anyway.

'Would you mind making your own way back to Tom Kemp's office?' Louis asked when they'd finished. 'I've got to . . . erm . . . see someone.'

Louis walked off towards the mansion in the dark, head down, hands thrust into his pockets.

The night was clear and although only a quarter moon hung in the sky, its silvery light was enough to reveal the potholes and other hazards as Daniel made his way back to the stable yard where he was to meet Tom in his office. Later, Mr Bullock, Gordon Welchman and Alan Turing would join them in the Swan pub. He made a mental note to pick up his slide rule which he'd left on Tom's desk.

As he rounded the side of the mansion, he was plunged into darkness and progressed slowly as he delved in his bag for a torch. But as he turned the corner, he was amazed to see Tom's office was bright with light, as if he'd completely forgotten to pull the blackout curtains.

It took him several seconds to realise the blackout curtains had indeed been pulled and the light was actually coming from them because one of them was on fire. As he watched, several of the window panes cracked and exploded, allowing flames to lick at the cold night air. It was the window behind which Tom usually sat at his desk, and Daniel had a mental image of the university don still seated, working, oblivious of the fire — or indeed, attempting to leave via the broom cupboard.

He ran towards the door, yelling 'Fire! Fire!' and taking a deep breath, he barged into the office.

Tom's desk was ablaze but luckily, there was no sign of him. Daniel glanced quickly around the door to the other end of the office but it appeared to be empty. He was just about to leave when he spotted a figure sprawled on the floor.

Rushing in, his lungs already bursting, he hoisted the figure into his arms and ran for the door, stumbling into the cold night. His eyes were streaming and he struggled to draw clean air into his lungs but thankfully, his cries had roused several people who ran towards the office with buckets of water and stirrup pumps.

Daniel recognised Tom in the stable yard, staring at the burning office in horror.

'Professor Kemp?'

'My spectacles! Did you see them?' he asked, 'They were on my desk . . . I need them.'

'No, I'm sorry. Look, I've got your assistant,' he said, amazed that Tom had taken no notice of the girl in his arms. Surely his eyes weren't so bad. But perhaps he was confused in the darkness with the roar of the flames and the shouts of the people who were trying to put it out.

'Jess!' Tom said in surprise. Looking at Daniel, he added, 'She needs to go to the sick bay!'

'Yes, I know. Where is it?'

'I'll take her,' Tom said in an unusual moment of decisiveness, then added, 'My stamp collection is in the top drawer of the file. If you could rescue it, I'd be very obliged — oh, and my spectacles.'

Daniel wondered if he was doing the right thing. If he'd known where the sick bay was, he'd have taken Jess himself, or passed her over to one of the soldiers who'd now joined the others and were putting out the fire. But Tom had slipped his arms beneath Daniel's and taken Jess's weight. Now, he was staggering across the stable yard holding the limp figure, walking with purpose as if he knew where he was going.

Daniel followed just to make sure he didn't get distracted, keeping out of

Tom's sight until he'd disappeared into the infirmary with the girl.

'Good gracious, lad! What on earth happened to you?' Mr Bullock said, leaping to his feet when Daniel finally arrived in the Swan, soot-streaked and smelling of charred wood.

'There was a fire in Tom's bunga-low,' Daniel said without explaining his involvement. Alan and Gordon threw their coats on, ready to rush off to see if they could help.

'Is anyone hurt?' Gordon asked.

'Tom's assistant is in the infirmary but I don't know how she is.'

'Are you all right?' Alan asked.

'Yes, I think so. And the soldiers are dealing with the fire.'

'I'm surprised Matron let you out of her clutches,' Gordon said.

'I didn't go to the sick bay.'

'Perhaps you should,' Alan said in concern.

'He's fine,' said Mr Bullock, clapping Daniel on the back. 'It's nothing a stiff whisky and a bath won't cure, is it, lad?'

7

Something was banging against Jess's head. Or perhaps the hammering was inside her skull. It was hard to decide.

She tentatively opened her eyes. Dark shapes danced against the brilliant light, rippling as if she were looking through water.

'Miss Langley?' a woman's voice said. 'You're quite safe. No need to worry. We're going to clean you up and make you comfortable. Just relax . . . '

Jess tried to reply but could manage only a croak. Her throat felt as if it had been sandpapered and it tasted as if she'd been chewing cinders. Her vision began to clear slightly and as the stinging receded, she realised she was in the sick bay with a nurse leaning over her. Sitting next to her bed, was Tom.

'It was lucky Professor Kemp was there to rescue you,' the nurse said, shaking her thermometer and putting it under Jess's tongue. 'Very lucky indeed. Although I've heard the fire is out now and no one else was hurt.'

Jess struggled to remember what had happened. The last thing she could recall was that she'd been working on a message, having managed to decipher the beginning. She'd worked on it for hours. In fact, all through the night. She'd stayed at work, certain she'd work out what the rest of the communication said eventually. Presumably, she'd fallen asleep at her desk and some time later, the fire had started.

She desperately wanted to thank Tom for saving her life but other than a grunt, she couldn't speak. Tom seemed to understand and patted her hand.

The nurse returned.

'I'm afraid you'll have to leave now, Professor Kemp, Miss Langley needs to rest. But I expect she'll be ready for visitors tomorrow.'

Tom nodded and after patting Jess's hand again, he left.

'The doctor should check him out too,'

the nurse said frowning as she watched him amble towards the door. 'He seems to be in shock.'

That's Tom behaving normally, thought Jess but her throat was too sore to attempt to explain.

* * *

Jess remained in the infirmary for the rest of the week and gradually, her voice returned to normal and her eyes no longer stung. Periodically, fragments of memory came back to her and she recalled waking to see a fire near Tom's desk.

She'd leaped up and must have fallen, knocking herself out against her desk, judging by the lump on the side of her head. Her ankle was swollen, so presumably she'd twisted that as she'd got to her feet in her bid to escape the flames. She remembered the heat... and the smoke and the feeling of helplessness and resignation.

The shock as she'd felt the cool, clear

air of the stable yard against her face also replayed in her mind and she recalled looking up through tear-streaming eyes into a face. Obviously, Tom's face as he rescued her. Then, she'd lapsed into unconsciousness. After that, there were no memories until she'd woken up in the infirmary.

Thank God for Tom. Without him and his bravery in getting her out of the fire . . .

★ ★ ★

'How's the patient?' Daniel asked Louis the following day when he met him in Alan's office.

'Tom's with her now. But she's fine, I think . . . '

'You think? Haven't you been to see her? I thought you two were good friends. In fact, I rather thought you two were a couple.'

'Jess and me?' Louis said, his cheeks heightening in colour.

'Well . . . yes. Sorry, I just assumed

. . . You always seemed to be together.'

'We work together,' Louis said.

'But you'd like it to be more?' Daniel asked.

'Lordy, no!' said Louis firmly.

'Sorry. I shouldn't have pressed you. It's really none of my business.' Daniel was horrified at his lack of sensitivity. But there was something so likeable about Louis, he felt he'd known him for years. Nevertheless, he'd overstepped the mark.

'It's all right, old chap,' said Louis. 'It was more the other way around, I'm afraid. But I'd be quite a disappointment to a lady . . . if you catch my drift.'

Daniel's confused expression showed he hadn't caught Louis's drift.

'Well, let's just say someone else has stolen my heart. Not that the feelings are mutual. But . . . ' He sighed. 'That's life, I suppose.'

Tom walked into the office, his hands full of papers and his spectacles perched on his head. A desk had been set up for him next to Alan's while the bungalow was renovated. Tom's side of the office had been most damaged and it was thought the fire had started there, probably in the waste paper bin or on his desk. It was probable that he'd caused the fire with a carelessly discarded match or his pipe. There had been plenty of paper piled on his desk and a bottle of whisky left over from Christmas, so once a flame had taken hold, there was plenty to keep it going.

He'd never found the pipe, although that didn't mean it had been on his desk and caused the blaze. After all, for some reason no one could explain, the spectacles he'd lost were later discovered in Hut 4. Despite his earlier remorse at probably starting the fire and his vow to give up smoking, he now had a new pipe clamped between his teeth.

'How's Jess?' Louis asked.

Tom blanched. 'All right, I suppose . . . under the circumstances. I told her it was probably my fault it started but she seemed very understanding. Thank God you found her,' he said to Daniel. 'If I were you, I'd go over to the sick bay and see her. I'm sure she'd like to thank you in person.'

* * *

Tom had been so sweet, Jess thought, with his head bowed and his hands clasped together. He'd mumbled his confession about starting the fire and had obviously expected her anger.

But it hadn't come as a surprise to her that his carelessness had been the cause. She found it more astonishing that his haphazard behaviour hadn't started a fire before. The only difference was that this time, after working for twenty-four hours, she'd been so tired, she'd fallen asleep at her desk and hadn't been able to react in time.

At least Tom had risked his life to rescue her. And somehow, they'd both survived. To his delight, the metal cabinet next to his desk had offered protection to its contents, including his stamp collection and as the bookshelf was nearer to Jess's desk than his, most of his books were intact although a few were drenched with water.

She knew he'd given up smoking in penitence and also knew his resolve would be short-lived. When he was focused on something, he didn't seem to realise what he was doing and it wouldn't be long before he came across another of his pipes and started smoking again. In fact, she thought she could see the tip of a pipe peeping out of his pocket.

There'd be no point getting angry with him. He couldn't seem to help himself. It would be like ranting at a puppy who had no idea its exuberance was unacceptable. In fact, it was a good analogy as his gentle eyes which appeared even larger behind his spectacles, betrayed every emotion. He'd stayed a while and read to her from a book which had a dirty cover and pages that were crumpled and stiff — obviously one that had been rescued from the fire — before suddenly realising he should have been at a meeting and rushing off. But his visit had been welcome — she was finding her enforced stay in bed tedious and she'd pleaded with him to bring her set of Dilly's Rods and some work to do, the next time he came.

The doctor had insisted on keeping her in for another day for observation after she'd got up, intending to find something to do, and passed out. He said she'd been exhausted, was suffering from shock and smoke inhalation, so he was insisting she remain in bed until further notice.

Gwen and Edna had promised to visit at lunchtime but as Jess looked up at the clock, there were still hours to wait. A nurse, arms piled high with fresh sheets, came back into the sick bay leaving the door ajar.

A man hovering outside took the opportunity to peek in. It was Daniel Matthews, the younger of the two men from the BTM Company. He spoke to the nurse and Jess heard her name mentioned.

Surely he hadn't come to see her?

What could he want? He was such a cold, standoffish man, she couldn't believe he'd come to enquire about her health. But the nurse was definitely heading towards her. She remembered he'd left a folder on her desk and his slide rule before the fire had started. Had he come to ask where they were?

She shut her eyes and pretended to be asleep. Through closed lashes, she watched the nurse return to Daniel, tucking a wisp of hair into her cap and smoothing her apron as she presumably told him Jess was sleeping. He turned to go but she called him back. Jess heard her giggling in a flirtatious way until Matron marched pointedly towards the door.

★ ★ ★

Daniel knew Jess had been awake when he'd arrived. He'd seen her glance at the clock above the door but as soon as she saw him, she'd closed her eyes.

Tom had been wrong. She hadn't wanted to thank him for rescuing her.

214

Not that he expected thanks, of course, but it seemed rude to ignore him after he'd risked his life for her.

As he went back to meet Mr Bullock, he reflected that his boss had been correct when he'd told him off for putting his own life in jeopardy.

'You'll get no thanks from the likes o' them upper-class girls, you know. And if something had happened to you, where d'you think I'd get a new assistant at short notice? You're too important to take chances with your life. You've got to think of the greater good, lad.'

Daniel hadn't said so but he thought Mr Bullock's comments heartless and crass. Saving a fellow human's life was surely of prime importance. But now he was beginning to wonder if his boss didn't have a point. After all, their relationship with Bletchley Park was beginning to bear fruit, and deciphering enemy messages with more accuracy would surely shorten the course of the war and determine a positive outcome. Suppose he'd been overcome by smoke and died?

Nevertheless, he couldn't possibly have walked away and left Jess in the burning office — even if she was one of those rude, aristocratic girls in pearls. But he'd been pleased Mr Bullock considered him an asset. He was normally sparing with his praise and Daniel had been trying hard to impress him, staying up late going over the electrical diagrams and making notes and drawings for the following day which he discussed with his boss over breakfast.

Several times, Mr Bullock had gone into Bletchley Park and put forward Daniel's ideas, then taken full credit. But, Daniel conceded, that was how business worked and if he didn't ultimately receive any recognition, well, at least he knew he'd contributed to the improvements of the BTM Company's Bombe Machines.

And unless something went wrong, there was still a chance Mr Bullock would put his name forward for promotion, as he'd once hinted.

8

Jess and Louis avoided each other as much as possible, although they were once again thrown together when she'd been discharged from the infirmary since she was now based in one of the cottages with Tom, Alan — and Louis.

They were polite to each other but Jess was sad that the friendship they'd enjoyed had gone. Socially, they didn't mix at all. Jess's ankle hadn't healed sufficiently to resume Scottish dancing although she'd continued with the Drama Group who were planning an ambitious production of Dido And Aeneas. She'd gladly handed the piano playing back to George Bancroft, whose hand had finally healed, and joined the chorus with Gwen and Phyllis. Louis had auditioned but before he could start rehearsing for his part, he'd announced he'd be going to one of Bletchley Park's outstations at Eastcote helping them set up their Bombe Machines.

Jess was sad but relieved he'd gone. It did, however, mean that the surly young man from the BTM Company was often in the office but Jess had very little to do with him. It was annoying because while he was there, various girls found excuses to come into the office to engage him in conversation. True, he never encouraged it. But it didn't stop the constant flow. He was a very good-looking man, Jess conceded, but there was more to romance than mere good looks.

She'd spent a lot of time with Tom since the fire. He'd taken her to the cinema and several concerts although on the last occasion, they hadn't made it inside the concert hall because he'd left the tickets at home. They weren't enjoying a romance in the way Jess understood the word, but then after losing her heart to Louis, she wondered if this safer, less intense feeling wasn't more sensible.

As well as seeing so much of Tom,

she'd often been to London with Gwen, Edna and Phyllis. Now Mr Connors, the head hall porter at Claridge's, greeted her by name and seemed to assume she was one of the Debs. They'd all been to the theatre on several occasions and had danced until the early hours on the famous raised dance floor at the Savoy.

Of course, work absorbed and drained her too. She was surrounded by wonderful people and life was full. Yet strangely, a feeling of fulfilment eluded her.

Perhaps her father had been right when he'd warned against self-indulgence — it might be as he'd said, very attractive but ultimately unsatisfying. Everyone around her seemed content — although perhaps they, too, were simply acting out a part as Jess seemed to be doing.

Or perhaps the uncertainty of war was undermining her peace of mind. The winter had been cold and they'd sat dressed in coats, hats and gloves at their desks during the worst of it in their freezing buildings with only a cast-iron coke stove which blew out long flames into the room when the wind was strong. Or, if it went out, it emitted billowing clouds of smoke, alarming Jess whose memory of the fire was still fresh.

And then again, perhaps she was simply exhausted.

★ ★ ★

At the end of March, Mavis Lever, one of Dilly's girls, deciphered a message to an Italian naval commander stating March 25 was 'today minus three'. Something major was obviously about to happen. The message was sent to the intelligence department, who deduced the Italian fleet was planning to attack British troop convoys sailing from Alexandria to Piraeus in Greece.

That information was sent to the Admiral of the Fleet who ordered the troop convoys to divert or remain at anchor and the Allied Mediterranean Fleet to set sail. It ambushed four Italian destroyers and four cruisers off the coast of Sicily, having, it must have seemed to the Italians, appeared from nowhere. The Allies were victorious at what was named the Battle of Matapan, only losing one torpedo bomber. The Italians lost over two thousand men — although the Allied ships rescued over one thousand Italian survivors.

How different the outcome would have been without Mavis Lever. The Italians generated very few messages, but it seemed they'd realised that if they suddenly sent a flurry of communications, the enemy might guess something was about to happen — even if they couldn't decipher the content. So the Italians regularly sent out dummy messages to make it look as though there was uniform transmission. One soldier had merely repeatedly hit the L button of his Enigma Machine, assuming he'd save himself some effort. However, he hadn't realised that miles away, Mavis was reading his message and she knew that when a particular letter is pressed, it would never be encrypted as itself. She spotted that among the groups of five letters, there was not one single occurrence of the letter L.

Using that clue, she and the others in the cottages worked for three days and nights until they'd cracked the entire message.

They were all exhausted but elated and Jess was particularly relieved because William was based in Alexandria. It was possible he'd been on one of those troop ships which were the target of the Italian Navy. Had Mavis not had the brilliance to spot an anomaly in an Italian message and had they not worked so hard . . . well, Jess couldn't bear to imagine.

Then there was more good news. A German trawler, Krebs, was captured in the Arctic Circle and yielded two Enigma machines and the Naval Enigma settings for the month of March. These only allowed the codebreakers to read retrospective messages. However, from all the tables and codes seized and other data, Alan Turing calculated a new method which allowed the workers in Hut 8 to break into enemy messages.

It wasn't until later that Jess realised

the U-boat attacks on the convoys in the Atlantic had decreased. During the first few months of 1941 Britain had faced catastrophic shortages of imported food and oil because of the repeated submarine attacks. However convoy re-routings based on intelligence from Alan Turing and his co-workers in Hut 8 were so successful that for the first twenty-three days of June, all the UK-bound convoys managed to evade the marauding U-Boats.

In May, there was more cause for cheer. A message was intercepted by Bletchley from one of the senior German military commanders in Berlin, requesting information from the German High Command about the battleship Bismarck, because his son was on board. The reply informing him the vessel was at Brest was intercepted and deciphered by Bletchley and shortly after, British warships attacked and sank the Bismarck, affecting morale in Germany. Hitler was reported to have been 'melancholy beyond words'.

All over Bletchley Park, small camp beds were set up in offices and huts so people could remain at their posts until exhaustion drove them to fall asleep and then on waking, to resume their work.

It was clear the work was vital to the war effort and that they desperately needed more staff and resources. There were now so many people working at the Park, trestle tables had to be set up in corridors, the air section took over the dining room and the ballroom was out of action because it was filled with tele-printers.

Winston Churchill, who'd followed closely the progress made by Bletchley Park, paid them a visit in September. Alan was so nervous, Jess thought he might actually hide away during the visit but he summoned the courage to show Churchill around Hut 8. After his tour of the site, the Prime Minister scram-bled on to a small mound outside Hut 6 and gave a short address to the gathered staff members. It was a grey day with a biting wind but Jess felt warm with pride when Churchill praised their dedication to the work and described them as 'the geese that lay the golden eggs — and never cackle.'

'Well, that's all very well,' Tom said after the Prime Minister had gone. 'But we're still understaffed.'

It was true. But after such a momentous visit, Alan, Gordon and several others felt sufficiently encouraged to write directly to Churchill informing him that the work was being held up or indeed, not addressed at all, because of staff shortages. They included a list of requirements which would allow Bletchley to work at maximum production — and each man signed the letter.

To their surprise and delight, Churchill's response was immediate — he told his Chief of Staff to make sure the people at Bletchley had all they wanted on extreme priority and to report to him when it was done. The written instruction was marked 'Action This Day'.

* * *

With Churchill's blessing, more funds were found for Bletchley Park and more people began arriving. The numbers of Wrens at the Park grew from hundreds to thousands, most brought in to operate the increasing number of Bombe Machines which were now housed in the new, blast-proof Hut 11. Another hut was already underway to accommodate more Bombes. With such an influx of machines, Louis was brought back from the outstation at Eastcote, and Daniel Matthews also was spending more time at the Park, supervising the installation and running of the equipment. His position as Mr Bullock's assistant was now permanent and he was trusted alone, leaving his boss to oversee the production of all the new Bombe Machines in Letchworth.

'Fancy a pint at the Swan tonight after work?' Daniel asked Louis when he first appeared back in Alan's office. 'You look like you need a drink.'

Mr Bullock wasn't good company in the evening but being on his own, Daniel had discovered, was even worse.

'So, how was Eastcote?' Daniel asked when Louis finally appeared.

'Passable, I suppose,' said Louis. 'A bit lonely, if I'm honest.'

'Yes, I know what you mean,' Daniel said.

'You? Lonely? I can't believe that. I lost count of the number of girls who wanted me to introduce them to you when I was last here. Don't tell me none of them appealed?'

'Well, it's not that none of them appealed, it's more that I've got to concentrate on my career before I consider anything else.'

'Really?' Louis's eyebrows shot up. 'What's more important than finding someone to love?'

Daniel explained about the responsibility he felt towards his parents and his aspirations to secure a good job and home.

'I understand wanting to repay your parents . . . well, actually, I don't, because my parents wrote me off years ago. But what's the point of a good job and home if you've no one to share it with?'

'Well, I hope to share it one day.'

'I'm amazed you can be so single-minded,' said Louis miserably. 'If I was lucky enough to have queues of people after me, I'd be happy.'

'Well, there are two Wrens over there looking this way,' Daniel said. 'Don't tell me they're not interested in you.'

'Sadly, old chap, it's a moot point. It seems to be you they're looking at, but even if not. . . well, let's say I'd be less than delighted. You see . . . I'm not too keen on the ladies . . . '

'Ah!' Daniel said in surprise.

'I understand perfectly, old chap, if you'd rather cut short our drinking session. I know men like me are rather frowned upon. Oh, and before you get the wrong idea, I'd like to make it clear that despite your Hollywood-style good looks, you're really not my type.'

'No, it doesn't matter to me,' Daniel said, 'but that makes your comments about Jess Langley much clearer.'

'Yes.' Louis shrugged and sighed.

'Poor Jess, I don't usually broadcast my inclinations but I assumed I must surely have given myself away to her. We spent quite a lot of time together. However, I think she is — was — a bit naïve and it turned out she had no idea. Even worse, she fell for me. She's such a sweet girl. I'm not sure what she's doing with Tom Kemp. They're not a good match at all. But each to his own. What would I know?'

'Jess Langley sweet? Really? She always ignores me. I thought she was rather rude. But I agree she and Tom are a strange couple.'

'So, Daniel, do tell me how you manage to resist all those offers of dates you pass up?'

'I must admit, it's getting harder and harder. But . . . '

'But what?'

'Well, I've spent years studying hard and then working to secure my job and I'm a bit . . . well, inexperienced.'

'Everyone's inexperienced until they get going.'

'Yes, I know — but I had an encounter with a girl from work and . . . '

Daniel told Louis about Sybil Mills. 'I didn't see it coming and once it had started, I couldn't stop. It all happened so fast. If her mother hadn't come home and it had all gone wrong, I could be married now with a child on the way. It all seemed so haphazard. I wanted something more meaningful for my life.'

'Well, it doesn't have to be like that. It's best to get to know someone first and then slowly build up to it,' Louis said with a laugh. 'Hark at me giving advice! My love life's non-existent!'

'I wish I could help.'

'Nothing to be done, old chap. But thanks anyway. You've certainly cheered me up this evening. I thought I had problems but you seem to have tied yourself up in knots.'

* * *

Daniel lay awake for some time thinking about the conversation he'd had with

Louis and his comment about tying himself up in knots. It was true. He'd been single-minded and determined for all the right reasons. But in striving to achieve so much, he'd focused on the journey without knowing what the destination would look like.

His parents were renting a cottage near his aunt in Essex and seemed happy to be out of London and the Blitz. He'd visited them several times and country life suited them. He'd also managed to send them more money each month because his salary had increased substantially with his promotion, and his future looked much brighter, with Mr Bullock increasingly relying on him. Had he reached his target without even noticing? If so, he could now relax a bit and start enjoying himself.

After keeping his emotions under such tight rein for so long, he wondered how to ease up.

But it was hardly a problem, he told himself. He'd done the hard work and now he could enjoy the benefits. Louis was unhappy with his lot, yearning for something he couldn't have — and poor Jess had fallen in love with him, longing for something he couldn't give her.

As he finally fell asleep, Jess's face was the last image in his mind. It was still there when he awoke in the morning.

★ ★ ★

The bungalow was finally ready for Tom and Jess to move back into the office. It smelled of new paint and fresh blackout curtains, but was as bare and austere as it had been before the fire. Tom lined up his books on the shelf and added several that he'd bought for Jess.

Louis was back working in Alan's office with some new members of staff, and Dilly had acquired several new girls who were working in his cottage. So when Daniel was at Bletchley, it was decided he'd be based in Tom's office. A new desk was carried in and placed near Jess's.

He spent most of his time in Hut 11

with the Bombe Machines but periodically, he found himself in the office with Jess and increasingly, he wondered what she saw in Tom. He'd begun to find it hard to concentrate on his work, his eyes being drawn upwards, off whatever he was reading, to study her face as she worked.

She wasn't beautiful, but small and delicate with rich, dark curls which framed a heart-shaped face and a fine complexion, like porcelain. There was nothing remarkable about her features. She wasn't his type at all. But somehow, he found her attractive and the more he peered at her over the top of whatever he was pretending to read, the more he was drawn to her. Every so often, she'd push her spectacles up her nose and he'd immediately lower his gaze.

It was pointless becoming interested in Jess. She'd made it clear she didn't like him and anyway, she was with Tom Kemp. And if that wasn't enough, she was, as Mr Bullock had once warned him, one of the Girls in Pearls who were out of his league. She mixed with many of Dilly's Fillies and Daniel had recently discovered that Jess's best friend, Gwen, was actually Lady Gwendoline Armstrong-Court. It seemed most of the Debs at Bletchley deliberately concealed their titles. It was only by chance Daniel had discovered Gwen's. So, presumably, Jess had a title too.

Marvellous! It seemed he'd given himself permission to take an interest in girls, only to find he was hankering after one who was out of his reach. Perhaps that was the point? Perhaps subconsciously he wasn't ready for a relationship so he'd settled on a girl who was unobtainable?

★ ★ ★

'Where d'you want this?' the man in overalls said as he pushed a sack barrow through the bungalow door. On it was perched yet another filing cabinet to add to their substantial collection.

Jess looked about the office. There was little space left. Tom glanced at his

234

bookshelf and sighed. It would have to go.

'Can't we move Daniel's desk further up?' Jess suggested.

Tom sighed again. 'There won't be any room for him to sit at it. We've already pushed it against the wall so he has to sit with his back to us.'

Jess had been relieved when Daniel's desk had been moved. On several occasions, she'd thought she'd caught him staring at her, although he rarely spoke to her other than to say what was polite or necessary. At least he was no longer as surly as he'd been when she'd first met him.

In fact, most of the time, he seemed to be in a daze but that wasn't surprising — everyone was exhausted although it was hoped that the new recruits arriving every day would offer some relief. It seemed they'd been toiling for months.

In fact, time seemed to have compressed to such an extent it almost seemed meaningless. Jess ate meals when she remembered and slept on the cot in the corner when exhaustion overcame her — the calendar on the wall was the only indication one day had merged into another.

'Jess? Jess?' Tom said.

'Mm? Sorry, Tom, what did you say?'

'The shelf has to be moved.'

'Yes, I suppose that's the only solution.'

'So, where shall we put it?'

Jess sighed and looked around the crowded office. 'How about cutting it in half and making two shelves which would fit over there?' She pointed above one of the filing cabinets.

'I knew you'd know what to do,' Tom said.

For such an intellectual, he was remarkably impractical. Sometimes it was as if she was the elder of the two. Or perhaps more like an adult dealing with a clever child.

'You look tired, Jess.'

She nodded.

'How about a picnic tomorrow?'

'I won't have time to prepare any-thing . . . '

'Leave it to me,' Tom said.

Jess was surprised. She wasn't convinced he'd manage, but was too tired to ask. It was October and not the usual picnic season, but if it meant time away from the office, she was in favour — although she'd actually planned a long sleep.

'We'll have to move Daniel's desk slightly,' Tom said as the man climbed on a chair to unscrew the bookshelf.

'Perhaps there's more room in Alan's office?' Jess asked hopefully.

Tom looked at her with a frown.

'Don't you like Daniel?'

'He's all right. He doesn't say much.'

'You don't say much to him,' said Tom. 'I've noticed . . . Only I would have thought there'd be some sort of bond between you.'

'Bond? What on earth d'you mean?' Jess laughed at the thought of anything connecting her to the sullen young man.

'Some people believe that if a person saves your life, you must repay them with yours. Like Friday became Robinson Crusoe's slave.'

'Are you saying I ought to become your slave?'

'No, not me! Daniel!'

'But Daniel didn't save my life!'

Tom blinked rapidly and stared at her.

'Of course he did. You can't have forgotten the fire . . . '

'But I thought you . . . '

'No, I took you to the sick bay. But it was Daniel who came in here and carried you out.'

* * *

'Here he comes!' said Phyllis, nudging Gwen.

'And he's got a picnic hamper and rug! Who'd have thought he'd remember!' marvelled Gwen.

'What — to come for Jessica or to remember to bring a picnic?' Phyllis asked.

'Although that hamper probably contains his stamp collection and chess set,' said Edna.

'Oh, stop it!' said Jess crossly, while

admitting to herself they were all correct in their assessment of Tom who was now walking up the drive to Lestcombe Hall. She'd checked with Phyllis's aunt that they could picnic in the grounds; she was certain Tom wouldn't know where to go and wouldn't have thought to find out.

She ran down to greet him, leaving the three girls on the landing looking out of the window.

'Won't you be cold?' she asked as she met him half way up the drive. The sky was clear but the wind was biting and he'd only put on a thick jumper and scarf. She'd wrapped up in coat, hat, scarf and gloves.

'I'm fine,' he said. 'Now where shall we go?'

So, he hadn't planned anywhere as she'd suspected. At least he'd turned up on time, dressed in day clothes and with a picnic basket — contents yet to be discovered. He'd certainly scored more points today than Gwen, Phyllis and Edna would have given him credit for.

Jess led him to the sunken garden, which she knew would be sunny and slightly screened from the breeze. He placed the rug and hamper on the grass, then she showed him around the grounds. They walked hand in hand and Jess felt his mind was really on her, and not thinking simultaneously of codes, ciphers and cribs.

'It'll be like this after the war,' he said, stopping to examine a bracket fungus on a tree stump.

'Like what? Peaceful?'

'Yes, but I was thinking of you and me together.'

'But Tom — once the war is over, we won't be together. Bletchley won't be needed and you'll go back to Cambridge. And I'll . . . well, I'll get a job in London or somewhere . . . ' She tailed off, realising she hadn't given her future much thought. So much mental effort was required for the present.

'No,' he said, 'we'll be married and you can't go to London to work. That's silly if you're living in Cambridge. And once the babies come along, you won't want to work, will you?'

She stopped and stared at him, her mouth wide open. 'Tom! Are you asking me to marry you?'

'Of course. We make a good team. I've got my own house just outside the city. Of course, it's nothing like this mansion but it's got four bedrooms and its own garden. It's a bit neglected but I know you'd do marvels there. You wouldn't be bored.'

Jess stared at him. Tom had proposed — well, sort of. She'd never thought about what a marriage proposal might be like but she was certain if she had, it wouldn't have been like this.

'You're not saying anything, Jess,' he said, blinking rapidly and looking at her anxiously, 'have I said the wrong thing?'

'No, no!' she said, 'It was a shock, that's all. Do you mind if I think about it?'

'Of course,' he said. 'No hurry. I can't see the war being over just yet. Take your time.' They wandered back to the picnic hamper and Tom lay back on the blanket, hands beneath his head, eyes closed, enjoying the sun. He was obviously leaving it to her to arrange the picnic.

Jess opened the lid and a blast of onion fumes assaulted her nostrils. She managed not to heave and opened the lid fully to allow the smell to be wafted away by the breeze.

'Cheese and onion sandwiches,' he said as he smelled the aroma. 'Mrs Chiddens did them for me this morning.'

Jess swallowed, tried not to breathe and put two sandwiches on his plate. She loathed raw onions. If he'd thought, he'd have known as the subject had come up before, with him describing at length how it was the action of cutting the onion and damaging the cells which released an enzyme which caused a chemical reaction resulting in the stink. He'd insisted on demonstrating and she'd gagged and narrowly avoided being sick.

'Not hungry?' he asked, taking an enormous bite of one of the sandwiches.

'No,' she said with a sigh, eyeing the

cake Tom's landlady had also packed. It would smell of onions too. She took the Thermos flask out of the hamper and poured them both tea.

* * *

'How was it?' Gwen asked later when Jess returned, 'Did he bring food?'

Jess nodded. 'Cheese and onion sandwiches.'

'I thought you loathed onion.'

'I do.'

'I think if you're going to continue to see him, you're going to have to get used to the idea his thoughts are always going to be elsewhere.'

Jess wondered whether to tell her about the unromantic proposal. She decided she would.

'Married? To Tom Kemp? Tell me you refused!'

'I didn't give him an answer.'

'Please tell me you're not considering it! He's a lovely man but emotionally he's a child. You'd spend the rest of your

243

life being his mother.'

Would that be so bad? she wondered later that night while she tried to sleep. Tom was kind and generous — even if he didn't know what she liked. But he'd provide for her, and they often had fun together. He saw the world in such an unusual way, he'd opened her eyes to all sorts of things.

But did she want to spend the rest of her life as a mother to Tom's children — and indeed, to Tom himself?

No, she decided, she couldn't marry Tom. She didn't know what she wanted to do, but it definitely wasn't to spend the rest of her life organising his.

She'd be unlikely to get a good job after the war because she couldn't account for her time at Bletchley. Her oath of silence would last forever. So how could she give a prospective employer details about her work experience?

Still, she'd get a job somewhere and at least she'd be independent and accountable to herself. Perhaps she'd travel. She'd always wanted to go to Switzerland,

Gibby's home.

And if the Nazis won the war . . . well, it wasn't possible to imagine what the world would be like.

Tomorrow, she'd tell Tom she couldn't marry him and try to extricate herself from their relationship — although exactly what their relationship was, she couldn't say.

They weren't sweethearts — not in the way she understood — but they seemed to be more than friends. But how to stop whatever it was between them? She didn't want to lose his friendship or cause any hostility. He was still her boss.

The reek of onion lingered in her nostrils even though she'd tried to mask it with precious drops of the Shocking perfume Louis had bought her.

She sighed and shook her head. The two men who'd featured greatly in her life were both represented by a smell. One whom she'd loved but wasn't interested in her, and the other to whom she'd grown closer following what she'd believed to be his dramatic rescue — except that he hadn't saved her life. He'd omitted to mention it had been Daniel Matthews who'd risked his life for her — and she hadn't even thanked him.

She'd effectively ignored him in the office and when he'd come to see her in the infirmary, she'd snubbed him by pretending to be asleep. Despite the aromatic reminders of Tom and Louis, it was Daniel's face which remained during her dreams.

Guilt, she thought as she awoke. As soon as she saw Daniel, she'd put that right.

9

Daniel noticed his desk had been moved again but this time, his chair had been placed so that he could see the office rather than facing the wall. The new filing cabinet and two smaller bookshelves were obviously the reason for yet another move and it was unlikely there'd be any more changes — there simply wasn't room.

Tom arrived soon after, smiling delightedly.

'Guess what? Jess and I are getting married.'

Daniel felt as though he'd been punched

'Congratulations, Tom. When's the happy day?' He didn't want to know but it seemed rude not to ask.'

Happy day?' asked Tom, rifling through a desk drawer absent-mindedly. 'What happy day?'

'Your wedding?'

'Oh, I see. No idea. I'll leave that to Jess . . . ' He pulled an ammeter out of the drawer. 'I wondered where that'd gone. Right, I'll be back in a jiffy. Better go and tell Dilly and his girls the good news . . . about the engagement, not the ammeter,' he said with a laugh, 'although I suspect Dilly'll be more pleased I've found his ammeter . . . '

Daniel felt sick with disappointment. It wasn't that he'd ever thought he stood a chance with Jess but he'd allowed himself to create all sorts of dreams about her, where she'd come to her senses and discovered she preferred him to Tom and wanted to be with him. It was out of the question, of course, but it had seemed to be a safe way of dealing with his feelings. Now he realised he should have been more realistic.

The door opened and Jess entered, her face lighting up when she saw him. He couldn't bear it. She was about to tell him her good news but he didn't want to hear it from her mouth.

'Congratulations,' he said, more abruptly than he'd intended. 'I hope you'll both be very happy.'

She frowned and tipped her head on one side.

'Congratulations? What for?'

'Tom told me about the engagement.'

Jess went white, her eyes widening, and he wondered if perhaps Tom should've warned him the couple wanted it kept secret.

She sank on to her chair.

'He actually said we were getting married?'

Daniel nodded.

'He proposed yesterday but I said I'd think about it.' Daniel dared not believe she was going to turn him down but he couldn't help himself.

'And are you going to marry him?'

Jess slowly shook her head.

'You might want to go over to Dilly's office because he's just gone to tell them the news,' Daniel said.

Her hand flew to her mouth and she jumped up, 'Oh no! I can't simply rush over there and contradict Tom. He'll look so foolish!'

'Well, it's either tell him or you might have to go along with it,' Daniel said, 'and I think you deserve better than that.'

He gasped as soon as he realised what he'd said but she was halfway out of the door and hadn't seemed to have noticed.

He decided to go for a walk. If Tom and Jess returned to the office, he didn't want to intrude. And he needed time to give himself a stern talking to. It didn't matter that she hadn't yet accepted Tom's proposal. He still might talk her round. And even if Tom didn't, there was still no possibility of Jess looking in his direction. She'd always been polite but aloof. Except for this morning, when she'd rushed in to the office and had seemed extraordinarily pleased to see him.

* * *

Jess's heels clattered on the cobbles of the stable yard as she raced to Dilly's cottage. How could she possibly contradict

Tom in front of Dilly, Gwen, Edna and whoever else was on duty? She couldn't make him look a complete idiot.

Yet how could she accept congratulations on a marriage which would definitely not take place? Had he done it to force her into accepting?

No, that wasn't possible. There was no guile in Tom. He'd probably simply forgotten he'd agreed to wait for her answer.

There was no guile in Tom. He was a good, kind man and he was the last person she'd ever want to hurt — and yet, she couldn't marry him out of pity or a sense of duty. Could she?

When she burst into the cottage, everyone was gathered around Dilly's desk and they looked up, startled at her abrupt entrance.

'Good news travels fast,' Dilly said, 'make some room and let Jess in.'

Mystified, she walked to the desk where a small space had been made for her.

'What luck, eh?' Tom said to her. 'Not only the machine but the tables and code books! All captured off a German trawler just off Norway by our lads!'

Jess looked at the battered Enigma Machine and assorted books, one of which appeared to be blood-stained.

'Right,' said Dilly, holding his hands up for silence, 'back to work, everyone. With these beauties we'll be reading Jerry messages to our hearts' content!'

'Well, at least until these codes run out,' someone said.

'Best hurry up, then,' said Dilly.

Jess followed Tom outside.

'Tom, you haven't told anyone other than Daniel about us getting married, have you?'

Tom slapped his palm to his forehead and groaned. 'I knew there was a reason I went to see Dilly . . . ' He turned to go back to the cottage.

'No, Tom, wait!' Jess grabbed his arm and pulled him towards the bungalow. 'I need to talk to you . . . It's just that when you asked me yesterday, I said I needed time to think . . . and I've thought . . . and I don't think it's a good idea.'

'Not now, of course.'

'No — not ever.'

Tom stopped and looked at her, his eyes wide in shock. 'Oh, I see.' He sighed and looked down.

'Perhaps we should talk about it some more,' he said after a few seconds' silence.

'No, Tom. I've made up my mind. I'm afraid it's out of the question — '

The telephone in the bungalow rang out and Tom hurried to answer it, leaving Jess outside. She felt wretched but relieved, though she wasn't certain he'd heard her say it was out of the question. But how much harder it would have been if he'd announced their engagement to everyone.

She followed Tom into the office where he was putting on his coat and hat.

'Something's come up,' he said but his voice was shaky.

'Tom? What is it? What's wrong?'

'We'll talk things over when I get back,' he said, patting her shoulder as he passed her.

'Get back? Where are you going?'

But he'd hurried out of the office.

She rushed after him. But he was striding away and she wondered if perhaps she ought to leave him. If he'd suddenly come to terms with her rejection, then he needed time to process it. And if it was something else, he hadn't thought to share it with her.

Knowing Tom, the telephone call could have been his landlady saying she'd knocked his half-finished chess game to the floor and he was going to put them all back in position.

Relief flooded into her. At least she'd have a while until Tom returned. With a start, she suddenly remembered she'd intended to thank Daniel for saving her life and explain why she hadn't done so before.

★　★　★

Jess checked Hut 11 but Daniel wasn't there, nor in the canteen. She decided to return to the bungalow via the mansion and see if he was in a meeting with Commander Denniston, but as she walked across the grass, she saw him on a bench down by the lake. He was sitting with his elbows on his knees and his chin on his hands, watching the swans glide across the water.

For a second, she wondered whether she ought to intrude but she couldn't put it off any longer. He must think her so rude and ungrateful.

He looked up and smiled when he saw her approach. But it was a sad smile, Jess thought. Was everyone upset today?

'Crisis averted,' she said, keeping her tone light. 'It seems Dilly's taken possession of a captured Enigma Machine as well as tables and code books. And when Tom saw them, he forgot to mention our supposed engagement.'

Daniel expressed delight at the newly acquired booty but she could tell his eyes were still sad.

'I'm sorry,' she said, 'I don't suppose you're the slightest bit interested that I don't want to marry Tom. I . . . I . . . actually came to apologise to you and to thank you.'

Daniel frowned and moved along the bench so she could sit down.

'An apology and a thank you?' he said but for the first time, his smile seemed genuine. Jess sat next to him and explained how only a few days before, Tom had mentioned in passing that Daniel had saved her.

'Apparently, now, I owe you everything. Much like Friday did to Robinson Crusoe.'

'I see. Well, I'm sure I can think of something you can do to repay the debt,' he said.

He was laughing at her but not unkindly and for the first time in a long while, she felt at ease.

'So how did Tom take the news?'

'It's hard to say. He rushed off somewhere and you know what Tom's like.'

Daniel nodded. He opened his mouth to say something and then changed his mind.

'I expect you were going to say Tom and I made a strange couple?' she said.

'You're a mind reader! But it's really none of my business.'

'The strange thing is, I'm not sure we are a couple at all. Not in the usual sense. But then, there's nothing usual about Tom. So it's hard to know how he's feeling now. I wouldn't say we were sweethearts. We were more like very good friends who happen to be a man and a woman. But that brings its own problems.'

'Why?'

'Because sweethearts break up. People recognise they're no longer together, and they meet other people and make new relationships. But with Tom and me . . . There's nothing to break up. We're friends and I don't want to stop being friends. Even if I did, it would be very awkward working in the same office. I think what I need to do is to try to find out how Tom sees our friendship and work out what to do from there.'

'Well, good luck with that,' Daniel said. 'He's not the easiest man to read.'

Jess leapt to her feet. 'I'm so sorry,

Daniel. I wanted to apologise for not thanking you earlier and here I am, pouring out my problems to you! I know you don't think much of me and I don't blame you but — '

Daniel stood up too.

'Don't think much of you? Of course I do — '

He paused as if he longed to say more.

For several seconds, they stared into each other's eyes, neither speaking. It was as if she'd met him for the first time. How could she not have noticed his blue eyes? How had she not seen the way the corners of his mouth tilted upwards?

The spell was broken when a group of Wrens came out of Hut 11 chattering. Daniel glanced over her shoulder and his eyes widened in alarm.

'Please feel free to say no but if you were serious earlier about doing me a kindness, I can think of one now,' he said keeping his voice low.

She was intrigued, 'Go on . . .'

'Hold my hand.'

'That's it?'

'Yes — one of the Wrens won't take no for an answer, so if she sees us together . . . '

Jess took his hand. She wondered if he wasn't exaggerating the Wren's interest in him. But she wanted to hold his hand. Had the relief of deciding she didn't want to marry Tom given her a sense of freedom? Whatever it was, she suddenly felt new, fresh and excited.

One of the Wrens looked over at them as the group walked by and on a whim, Jess stood on tiptoe and brushed Daniel's lips with hers.

She expected him to look at the Wren to check her reaction, but instead, he locked eyes with Jess placing his other hand on the small of her back, then leaned towards her.

Their lips met again and it seemed to Jess everything had stopped. There was no sound, no cold breeze, nothing, just his lips on hers and the sensations which rippled through her body.

He broke away and looked at her in wonder.

The Wrens had gone.

'What just happened?' she whispered.

'I think,' he said, 'I overstepped the mark.'

'It seems I started it,' said Jess, amazed at herself for her boldness. Had she gone mad? If she had, it felt wonderful.

★ ★ ★

'Now what?' Daniel asked when they arrived back at the bungalow.

Jess shrugged. 'You've been part of my world for long enough to guess I don't have a clue. I expect you've much more experience than me in these sorts of matters. You always seem to have girls hanging around you. What do you suggest?'

Daniel shook his head.

'I suspect I have less idea than you.'

'Well, I suppose when all else fails, we could try honesty. It would save us a lot of time.'

Jess was amazed at how seriously she'd misjudged Daniel. She'd been touched

260

at his determination to succeed in the BTM Company so he could help his parents, to the exclusion of having fun and finding a girl.

He'd been sympathetic when she'd told him about her cold parents and how the only member of her family she felt close to was William.

'But over the last few weeks, I've felt drawn to you — even though I knew you were with Tom. I never intended to let you know. And I even wondered if I'd picked you because you were unattainable . . . .'

'And now?' she asked, fearing he'd say he'd made a mistake.

'And now, if you were my girl, I'd be the happiest man in the universe.'

'I'd love to be your girl . . . but I need to see Tom first and make sure he understands.'

'So you're my girl in secret until you tell Tom?'

She nodded.

He held out his hand as if to shake it but when she clasped it, he smiled, pulled her to him gently and wrapped his arms around her.

'Let's start as we mean to go on and seal it with a kiss,' he whispered.

★ ★ ★

1942

'You're looking rather pleased with yourself these days,' Edna said as she peered over the top of her teacup at Jess. 'Anyone'd think you had a secret sweetheart.'

'As if she'd have time!' Gwen said quickly.

Jess had only told Gwen and Phyllis about Daniel. Edna couldn't keep a secret and until Tom returned, it was best she didn't know. The telephone call he'd received after Jess told him she couldn't marry him had been a call to his mother's bedside, ostensibly to say goodbye, but Mrs Kemp had rallied on her son's return and Tom had remained at home with her, travelling to Letchworth to assist Doc Keen and his team.

He'd appeared at Bletchley on several occasions but not for long enough for Jess to talk to him.

'Pass the toast,' Edna said, appearing to lose interest. After all, Gwen was right. Unless a girl worked with her young man, like Mavis Lever, the girl who'd deciphered the Italian message and saved the troop ships at the Battle of Matapan, it was hard to conduct a social life outside of Bletchley. Mavis was seeing one of her co-workers, Keith Batey, and it was rumoured they were about to get engaged. Jess hadn't seen Tom for some time and Edna would have known if there'd been someone else, she was certain.

They were all so busy and so tired, and it wasn't as if things were getting any easier. The harder they worked, the more there was to do. At the end of 1941, the Allied campaign to eject the Germans and Italians from North Africa had been going well, with the capture of Benghazi on Christmas Day. But in early 1942, General Rommel had struck suddenly, forcing the Allies back almost to where they'd begun.

Shortly after, Singapore had fallen to the Japanese. And another disaster occurred — one which very few knew about, but which threatened the work of Bletchley Park. Admiral Dönitz became suspicious that somehow his codes were being read and introduced a fourth rotor on all of the U-Boat Command's Enigma Machines. Immediately, people at Bletchley found they could no longer decipher any U-Boat messages and work began anew to find a way to crack the codes. Meanwhile Atlantic convoys were once again vulnerable to attack, with countless crew members perishing in the hostile seas and vital supplies being sent to the ocean bed.

There was still an uphill struggle at Bletchley and the further they climbed, the steeper it got.

'See you outside in ten minutes,' Edna said, wiping the corners of her mouth with a serviette.

When she'd left, Gwen nudged Jess.

'I don't know how you've managed to keep it from Miss Nosey for so long!'

'I suppose it's because we don't actually get together very often,' said Jess with a sad smile, 'and now Daniel's gone back to Letchworth for a while, I won't see him at all.'

Gwen patted her shoulder sympathetically,

'Well, at least he's not in much danger . . . ' She broke off and Jess placed her hand on her friend's. Both knew Gwen was thinking of William out in North Africa with General Montgomery's forces.

'Men,' said Phyllis with forced jollity, 'honestly, they're nothing but trouble.' She put her arms around them both and hugged them tightly.

* * *

Daniel was now part of Doc Keen's team — not just an assistant but an engineer in his own right. Mr Bullock no longer kept a fatherly eye on him and had even

265

hinted that now he'd risen so high in the company, it might be time to settle down.

'You've shown yer dedication, lad. Well, after that dubious incident with the Mills floosie, anyway.'

He'd laughed at Daniel's crestfallen expression.

'You knew about that?' Daniel asked, appalled.

'Tony Sinclair made sure I knew all about you and the infamous Sybil Mills,' Mr Bullock said, 'but, to be honest, by the time he'd told me, you'd already made yerself invaluable. And as for Sinclair . . . he's not to be trusted.'

He'd even suggested introducing Daniel to his niece. There would be no obstacle to Daniel finding a girl.

'Thanks, Mr Bullock, but I've got my eye on someone,' Daniel said.

10

Jess was the first downstairs to check the post. There was a letter addressed to Gwen from William and another to her, in Daniel's writing, as there was each morning. Holding it to her nose, she breathed in the aroma of oil which accompanied his letters.

It was a thoroughly unpleasant smell, one that filled Hut 11, which was crowded with Bombe Machines. The Wrens who operated the Bombes complained bitterly about the hot, black oil that dripped on the floor from the rotating drums and Jess was always glad to get out of the dingy, stinking hut. But the barest whiff of oil on the paper told Jess that Daniel had written to her from work. He'd been thinking of her even while he'd been busy, and had either remained after work to write or written snatches during the day. It seemed to be proof that, as he'd told her, she was always on his mind.

'I long to tell everyone we're a couple but I don't want to risk hurting Tom's feelings,' Jess had told Daniel on one of his fleeting visits to the bungalow. 'I'm not sure how he feels about me now. But I didn't want to take the chance I'd upset him if he does feel anything for me. Especially while his mother's ill.'

'Even if everyone knew, it wouldn't help us spend more time together. We're never in the same place at the same time. But I don't want people to think we're seeing each other behind Tom's back. I don't mind for myself, but I don't want people thinking badly of you,' Daniel had said loyally.

'We'll just have to wait for him to come back and then I'll talk to him.'

Jess had looked down at the pile of papers on her desk, each covered in sets of five letters. By the end of the day, she'd either have made sense of them, or not. But at least it would be clear if she'd succeeded or failed.

Her work was governed by rules. Rules about setting up the Enigma Machines, rules about the way they functioned and rules about how to break the codes. Why wasn't life clear like that? If her parents had blamed her to her face for Clara's death, she would at least have known how they felt. She would have had chance to tell them how she felt. But it was never discussed. Now, she was afraid to hurt the feelings of a man who she wasn't sure even remembered she existed.

He'd not contacted her or replied to her letters. She'd told him she would not marry him. So why couldn't she just move on? Her world seemed full of shadows. And how could she fight a shadow?

'Jess? Jess! Are you all right?' It was Daniel leaning towards her, concern in his eyes.

'Yes,' she'd said sadly. 'I'm just dealing with shadows.'

'You needn't deal with them alone, you know.'

She'd smiled and pretended his words had cheered her. In the end, that was exactly what she had to do, she thought. If she couldn't fight her own shadows, how could he?

'Anyway, I was asking you if you came by bicycle today?'

Jess had nodded.

'I'll be waiting for you outside when you've finished work,' he'd said and that night, he'd taken her bicycle and wheeled it home with her through the dark roads. They'd held hands all the way, their gloves off despite the frost, so they could interlink their fingers and enjoy the touch of each other's skin, even if it was only the palms of their hands. They'd stopped every so often and Daniel had wrapped his arms around her and they'd kissed — long, lingering kisses which had ignited something inside her. She'd unwrapped her scarf and undone her coat to allow his kisses to continue down her neck but despite the warm glow inside, the vicious wind chilled her and Daniel had reluctantly rebuttoned her coat and wrapped her scarf around her neck.

'I'm not going to be responsible for

you catching double pneumonia,' he'd said with a sigh.

She'd wondered if she could smuggle him into the kitchen in Lestcombe Hall but when she'd opened the door to see if the way was clear, Mrs Jenner was there enjoying a cup of tea before bed. There was rarely an opportunity to be alone — and if there was, invariably they were bundled up in many layers of clothes against the cold.

★ ★ ★

'Jess! Are you planning on reading that letter, or inhaling it?' Gwen asked, taking William's letter and slipping it in her bag. She'd come down the sweeping staircase without Jess noticing. 'If I were you, I'd stop sniffing and put it in your pocket quickly, Edna'll be down in a minute and Phyllis is outside in the car waiting for us.'

At the entrance to Bletchley Park, the sentry crouched down to see who was in the shooting brake Phyllis was driving.

271

'The usual crew?' he asked good-naturedly.

'Yes, Sergeant. Edna, Jessica, Gwen and myself.'

'Righty-ho. Oh, I nearly forgot. I've a message for Jess Langley. She's to see Miss Abernethy as soon as she arrives.'

'Any idea why, Sergeant?' Phyllis asked as Jess got out of the car.

He tapped the side of his nose. 'Top secret! But all I'll say is, ladies, watch out for the Yanks.'

★ ★ ★

Jess knocked on Commander Denniston's door. Miss Abernethy opened it immediately and ushered her in.

'Jess, I'd like you to meet Captain Hunter of the United States Army.'

'Good to meet you, Jess,' the captain said, shaking her hand with a firm grip.

A few weeks before, in December, an agreement had been signed in Washington between Britain and the USA which would allow both countries to exchange technical information about German, Italian and Japanese codes. The arrival of this small group of Americans was the first attempt at collaboration. It was also the first time many of the people at Bletchley, including Miss Abernethy, had met an American.

Captain Hunter was tall and broad-shouldered — almost larger than life, Jess thought. With his chiselled features and dark, closely cropped hair, he reminded her of a Hollywood film star and she noticed Miss Abernethy was staring at him too. His voice, slow and deliberate with such an intriguing drawl, filled the room.

'Call me Chuck, please. I understand you Bletchley folks don't stand on ceremony.' He smiled, showing even, white teeth. With his health and energy, it was obvious he wasn't a man who was used to the food rationing and deprivation being experienced in Britain.

Miss Abernethy blinked and appeared to awaken from a trance. 'Chuck, er yes, of course, sir.' She looked at Jess and finally summoned her usual business-like tones. 'Since Tom Kemp isn't here at the moment, Captain . . . er, Chuck . . . will be working in the bungalow with you, Jess. Perhaps you'd give him a quick tour of the Park and make sure he has everything he needs.'

Chuck told her he'd arrived with four Americans the day before to set up a close relationship with the codebreakers at Bletchley and their counterparts in Washington. As Jess showed him around, he took an interest in everything. And the many women they encountered took even more of an interest in him.

'He's like a Greek god!' one Wren whispered to her friend as they stood against the the corridor wall to allow Chuck and Jess to pass, clipboards clutched to their chests and mouths open.

Jess showed him the newly-completed Hut 11A which was about to be fitted out with more Bombe Machines. Mr Bullock and Daniel would be arriving with the consignment and would oversee the installation.

'And this is Hut 11 where the Bombe Machines are now,' she said, opening the door for Chuck.

'Impressive,' he said as he wandered about, admiring the machines with their whirring drums.

Several of the Wrens operating the Bombes nudged each other, smiling at the tall, dark visitor.

One walked towards Jess, her lip curled in contempt. 'Blimey! You can't 'elp yerself, can you? For such a mousy little thing you seem to have yer claws into a lot of men. Tom Kemp, Daniel Matthews and now . . . ' she glanced admiringly at Chuck. 'Anyone else? It might be good manners to leave some men for the rest of us!' She barged into Jess as she passed and looked back over her shoulder at Chuck.

'Friend of yours?' Chuck asked in a slow drawl when they were outside.

'No, not really,' Jess whispered. Her cheeks were crimson with humiliation. She recognised the Wren as Sally, the one Daniel had wanted to avoid when she'd first kissed him.

'I didn't think so,' Chuck said with a laugh.

Jess finished the tour after introducing him to Dilly's Fillies in the bungalow and showed him Tom's desk.

'This is swell, Jessie, thanks. I have a few calls to make, then I'm meeting the others in my party.'

She smiled, nodded and shuffled the papers on her desk.

He picked up the telephone receiver, regarded her with a frown and put it back in its cradle.

'You're not letting that girl get to you, are you?'

Jess swallowed and shook her head. 'I'm embarrassed about what people'll think of me.'

'Who cares?'

'I do,' Jess said in a small voice.

'So, go and slap her smug face or whatever it is you British girls do in such situations.'

Jess laughed. 'We certainly don't slap people!'

'Well, maybe you should!' His eyes twinkled.

'You're laughing at me, aren't you?'

'Well, maybe just a little.'

What was it about this man that made him so easy to talk to? 'But if it bothers you that much, go and tell her,' he said. Jess hung her head. Until she got Tom's blessing to move on, then as far as everyone else was concerned, she was guilty of seeing two men at once.

'It's complicated,' she said. 'A bit like trying to fight shadows.'

'That's easy,' he said, snapping his fingers.'Just turn the light on. Shadows either disappear in the brightness or stand out intensely. Don't put up with any nonsense, Jessie. Make it plain what you want . . . or what you don't want. People usually listen to reason.'

Jess looked at him uncertainly.

'Jessie, if the world offers you a deal you don't like, negotiate some more until it's exactly what you want.'

In Chuck's world, Jess was certain people did listen to reason and if they didn't, they'd be open to negotiation. And the advice he'd given her was intended to prompt her to tell the Wren to leave her alone. But before she did that, she'd have to sort out the problem of Tom . . .

It suddenly seemed so simple. She'd ask for leave and go and see him.

★ ★ ★

On the first opportunity to take leave, Jess caught the earliest train to London, arriving at Tom's mother's house in west London late afternoon. Tom opened the door and his face lit up when he saw her.

'So,' he said when he'd led her into the conservatory and moved a pile of newspapers from a chair for her, 'what brings you to London?'

Jess swallowed, 'Tom, you know I'll always think of you as a dear friend . . . '

Tom looked confused.'

But I've fallen in love, and I wanted to tell you in case . . . that is, I hoped you wouldn't mind . . . '

'Mind? Jess, that's wonderful news! Who's the lucky man? Now, let me guess! It would be Donald, wouldn't it?'

'Donald?'

Tom thought for a moment. 'You know, the man from the BTM Company.'

'Do you mean Daniel?'

'Yes, Daniel, that's right.'

'But how did you know?'

'It's obvious you two are made for each other.'

'But, Tom, the last time you were there, I wasn't even talking to him.'

Tom tipped his head and frowned. 'Yes, now you come to mention it, you didn't seem to like him very much. All's well that ends well, eh?'

'And you don't mind?'

'Mind?' Tom looked at her in surprise. 'Why on earth should I mind?'

'The last time we were together, you proposed.'

'And as I remember, you turned me down.'

'Well, yes, but I wasn't sure you

279

believed me.'

'I think, Jess, it would've been a disaster if we'd married. I realised that later. There are places inside my head I still haven't explored. There are thoughts I need to discover and truths I need to search for. You deserve a man whose thoughts are all about you. I couldn't be that man.'

'I'm not quite sure what you mean, Tom, but I think that may be the sweetest thing anyone's ever said to me.'

Tom beamed.

'So, did you come to tell me about Donald?'

'Daniel. And yes. I didn't want to upset you.'

'Good gracious, Jess, you could've written and saved yourself the journey.'

'I wrote to you several times but you never answered.'

'No, I don't suppose I did,' Tom said, cleaning his glasses on his tie. 'Oh well. Now you're here, come and meet Nurse Phillips. What a marvellous woman! I engaged her to look after Mother but it's been wonderful having her here. Do you know, she's nursed in some of the poorest areas in India and China? Such stories she tells ... '

And that's that, Jess thought as she left Tom's mother's house. As easy as turning on the light.

She stopped at a telephone box, found some coins and dialled Daniel's work number.

'Hello, Daniel, I'm in west London, I've just been to see Tom and he's perfectly fine about us. In fact, I think he's got a bit of a crush on his mother's nurse. What time d'you finish work?'

'Jess! What a wonderful surprise! What time's your last train back to Bletchley?'

'It's not for hours.'

'Can I take you to dinner?'

'I was hoping you'd ask that.'

* * *

Daniel slipped his hand into hers as several people came out of the entrance to the BTM Company and stared.

'Who's the lucky lady?' one of the men asked.

'This is Jess, my sweetheart,' Daniel said before they walked off to the restaurant.

'I don't know why I didn't go and see him before, instead of waiting for him to come back . . . Well, I do know. I didn't think I'd get a straight answer. It was always so hard holding a conversation with him if he didn't want to discuss something.'

'So, how did you do it?'

'Well, let's say somebody told me to re-negotiate until I liked the deal. So I was determined to stay with Tom until I was sure he understood and accepted it. In the end, it took less effort than I'd expected.'

The restaurant was dark with candles on each table and a log fire which blazed brightly, filling the room with warmth and the aroma of pine.

'Well, this is unusual,' Daniel said as he helped Jess out of her coat in the restaurant. 'We're usually dressed for Arctic conditions, either at work in that freezing office or walking home. I wonder if I'll recognise you when we're wearing summer clothes!'

'So, you still expect us to be seeing each other in the summer?' she asked in a joking tone which masked her anxiety. He'd never mentioned the future before.

'Of course! And for many summers to come.' He looked at her nervously to see if she agreed.

'I want that more than anything.'

Daniel led her to a quiet table in the corner.

Jess unbuttoned her cardigan and began to blush as she saw Daniel watching her intently.

'Do you know, I've never seen — let alone touched — your arms,' he said, his voice husky.

Removing a cardigan was such an ordinary thing — usually done without thought — but now, Jess felt surprisingly shy as Daniel watched.

'My arms are nothing special,' she said timidly, allowing the cardigan to slip on to the chair. 'I mean, they're just the same as everyone else's.'

'Nothing about you is the same as anyone else, Jess,' Daniel murmured as he took her hand across the table and stroked her wrist with his fingertips. The orange glow from the flickering candle reflected in their faces then blended into the dimness, creating the illusion they were alone in a world which had suddenly and surprisingly become intimate.

The sensations running up her arm as Daniel continued to caress her wrist quickened her pulse and she found she was holding her breath while deep inside, she seemed to be melting. The simplest of pleasures had been denied them for so long. She'd never before felt his fingers brush her arm, nor seen the bulge of his muscles beneath his shirt. They were things one might ordinarily take for granted. But Jess's senses were heightened.

If she felt so aroused now, as he simply stroked her wrist, what would it be like to lie next to him? Jess burned with desire to find out.

'I wonder if this is what it's like for Eskimos?' Daniel whispered. 'How intense it must be when they finally get a chance to peel off the layers to see and touch the one they love.'

Love?

'Yes, Jess. I did say 'love',' he said, reading her thoughts. 'You must know I love you.'

'Oh, Daniel, I love you too!'

'It's so wonderful to have you to myself for a change,' Daniel said after their meal. He checked his watch. 'We'd probably better go. It's a fair walk to the station.'

'Are we far from where you live?'

'It's just around the corner. That's how I know about this restaurant.'

'Can we go and see your rooms?'

'Now?' Daniel asked in surprise. 'Well, we could just about manage it but we'll have to run if you're going to catch your last train.'

'I was thinking of catching the milk train back to Bletchley in the morning.'

Daniel took her hand and held her gaze.

'Are you sure, Jess? We don't have to do anything you're not comfortable with.'

'I want to do this, Daniel. More than anything.'

'Are you sure you don't want to wait until . . . well, until . . . ?'

'Until what? We've no idea what life's going to throw at us. I don't want to wait any more.'

'I just wanted our first time to be perfect.'

'It will be,' said Jess firmly.

'There's just one problem. My landlady doesn't allow her tenants to have guests overnight, so we'll have to be very quiet.'

Why had she promised it would be perfect? He'd been vague about previous girlfriends but a man who'd had so many girls after him would undoubtedly know exactly what to do, as well as what she should do. She'd be a terrible disappointment. Why hadn't she waited as he'd suggested?

She only had to tell him she was afraid and she knew he wouldn't push her. But she couldn't. She didn't want to let him down.

As they approached his house, he groaned softly.

'That's my landlady.'

A stick-thin woman had just opened the door to a man who was asking about renting a room. She nodded at Daniel and glared at Jess before telling the man the room had gone and closing the door.

Daniel sighed. 'She'll be waiting in the hall. There'll be no getting in there tonight. If we hurry, we'll make it to the station for your last train. Or we could find a hotel . . . ' But before she could reply, he added, 'No! I want our first time to be special, not in some grimy hotel room.'

'I love you, Daniel.'

'I love you too, Jess. And I'll see you on Friday at Bletchley. Perhaps we can make plans then.'

On Friday, Daniel rushed into the bungalow and leaned over Jess's desk to kiss her. 'I've got to be quick, I took a detour via the stable yard on my way to Hut 11. Doc'll get there before me if I don't hurry but I wanted to come and see you first.' He kissed two fingers and touched her cheek. 'I'll be back later. Don't go anywhere! Promise me!'

Jess caught his hand, kissed it then let him go.

Don't go anywhere? The pile of papers in front of her was so high, she'd be there all day without getting to the bottom of them.

'I'll be here,' she said, smiling at him as he rushed out. How could one man make the dingy office with its single lightbulb light up so brightly? And how dismal and dreary it was when he'd gone. For so long her life had seemed as random as the encrypted messages — strings of letters but meaningless without the key to decrypt them. Daniel was her key. With

288

him by her side, everything in her life fell into place and made sense. She was accepted, loved unconditionally and no one else's opinions about her mattered.

* * *

Jess took off her spectacles and rested her head on her hands, then, closing her gritty eyes, she massaged her temples. Some people's experience of war work was dangerous and frightening — firefighters who tackled the blazes after bombing raids, nurses tending to soldiers near battlefronts, all the soldiers, sailors and airmen . . . Her work, on the other hand was not dangerous nor frightening. It was monotonous, dull, painstaking and at times, downright frustrating, she thought crossly. She'd spent all morning trying to decipher a message which at first had seemed within reach but it continued to elude her. And Daniel still hadn't returned.

There was a sound from outside and she looked up and put her spectacles back on. Daniel entered, holding something she couldn't see behind his back. He was smiling, that lopsided, excited, little-boy smile she loved.

'Here!' he said and placed the Enigma Machine he'd been holding behind his back, on her desk.

She looked up at him with a frown.

'Is that Dilly's?'

He nodded happily.

'You realise what he'll do to you if he discovers you've taken it out of his office?'

Daniel nodded again, grinning even more.

'Well, open it and I'll be able to take it back!' he said excitedly.

It would be just like Daniel to have placed a rose inside, although where he'd have got a rose from, she had no idea. She lifted the lid. There was no flower, nor anything else inside.

'Here!' he said, pulling a sheet of paper out of his pocket and placing it front of her. On it were written eleven letters — YAEON LQXSA P.

'I've set up the rotors, just type the encrypted letters in,' Daniel said eagerly.

Jess pressed the Y key and on the top of the machine, the letter M was illuminated.

'Carry on!' said Daniel.

When she'd finished typing the letters and had written down the decrypted message, she looked up at him with tears in her eyes.

'Yes! Oh, yes!' she said. The decrypted message read MARRY ME JESS.

She rushed around the desk and clung to him as someone tapped on the window. Outside, visible through the criss-cross of the tape on the window panes were Dilly and what appeared to be all his girls, cheering and waving.

'I asked them for some privacy!' Daniel said ruefully. 'That would have been very embarrassing if you'd said no . . .'

'Say no? Daniel Matthews, I'd follow you to the gates of Hell if necessary.'

As he kissed her, the cheers from outside in the stable yard grew in volume.

'You're engaged to Daniel? But what about poor Tom?' Edna asked, stirring her tea at breakfast, 'I thought you and he were unofficially engaged.'

'How did you know that?' Gwen asked.

'Edna knows everything.' Phyllis laughed.

'She didn't know about Daniel,' said Gwen triumphantly.

'I would appreciate it if you wouldn't talk about me as if I wasn't here,' Edna said, sipping her tea. 'And no, I didn't know about Jess and Daniel. To be honest, it wouldn't have occurred to me she had it in her. Two men on the go at the same time is a bit . . . well, fast, for my liking.'

'Now you're talking about me as if I'm not here,' said Jess. 'I didn't have two men on the go at the same time, as you so delightfully put it, Edna. It wasn't like that at all. And as for 'poor' Tom, he's fine. He's head over heels in love with his mother's nurse.'

'Well, if you say so.' Edna sniffed.

'But in my opinion, your behaviour's outrageous. Honestly! When I first met you, Jess, you seemed to be such a ninny. I don't know what happened to you but you've changed. There's even talk about you and that very handsome American captain you're often seen with.'

'Nonsense!' Gwen snapped. 'It's people like you who start nasty rumours! Why don't you mind your own business?'

She walked briskly out of the morning room.

'Well done, Edna!' Phyllis said shaking her head in exasperation.

'What did I say?' Edna asked innocently. 'I'm entitled to my opinions, you know. And it's not my fault Gwen seems to be so bad-tempered at the moment. For the last few days all she seems to do is snap.'

'She's just tired. We're all tired,' said Phyllis, 'and if you want a lift into work this morning, you'd better apologise to Gwen and Jessica. I don't intend to drive to work with everyone at loggerheads.'

'All right, all right!' said Edna crossly.

'Don't blame me if other people are being touchy.'

'So, where's your apology?' Phyllis asked.

'Sorry, Jess.' She obviously wasn't sorry but presumably, the prospect of walking to work was much less appealing.

'You'd better find Gwen before we leave!' Phyllis called after her, then turning to Jess, she whispered, 'And I hope Gwen accepts her apology. She's on a bit of a short fuse at the moment, isn't she?'

'Edna's always on a short fuse — '

'No, I mean Gwen. She's usually so placid but just lately, she's very prickly.'

'I think she's missing William. He hasn't been home for weeks and she hasn't had a letter either. I must admit, I'm worried sick too.'

Phyllis sighed. 'When will this dreadful war be over and we can start living without the threat of death and destruction?'

11

Jess lay on the bunk, her head spinning and her stomach churning. The seasickness was bad enough but the disappointment was much worse. She'd been looking forward to working in America since Chuck had suggested that Jess as well as Peggy and Doris, two of Dilly's girls, went to Washington to share techniques with the American cryptanalyst team. Doc Keen had been invited along as well and he'd suggested Daniel go with him. Mr Bullock had been angry he'd been passed over and had not been mollified when Doc told him he was needed in England. Jess had a few anxious days while a decision was made by the board of the BTM Company until she heard Daniel would be going to Washington too.

'If we like it out there, p'raps when the war's over, we could return and live there,' Daniel had said as he walked her back to Lestcombe Hall.

'What about your parents?' Jess had asked knowing how attached he was to them.

'They can come too. Chuck told me the land is cheaper out there — well, not in the middle of Washington, of course, but further out into the country. I'll build them a house. At last, I'll be able to thank them properly.'

Jess had met Mr and Mrs Matthews. She'd been nervous but they'd been so welcoming and accepting — loving, even. Perhaps in time, they might become like parents to her. Certainly no one could do a worse job than her own parents.

And then the news had come that the Bombe Machines which had just been delivered and installed at Bletchley had developed a fault. Doc, Mr Bullock and Daniel were needed to investigate and no one would be leaving for Washington until they were running properly.

'I'm not going without you,' Jess had said.

'Jess, if you don't go with the group,

there's a danger they won't let you follow — and then I'll be out there and you'll be stuck here.'

In the end, she'd agreed, hoping they'd miraculously mend the Bombes and at the last minute, join the ship before it sailed.

But the men had to wait for a part to be manufactured and fitted before they could test the Bombes, by which time, the ship had sailed.

'We'll be over as soon as possible,' Daniel had said.

★ ★ ★

Jess had never seen anything like the wide boulevards of Washington, laid out in a grid around Capitol Hill. She longed to explore the city and the river banks but decided to wait until Daniel arrived.

Finally, word came that Daniel and Doc had boarded the SS Eloquence and were on their way.

On the day the ship was due to dock, Jess couldn't concentrate on work.

'Jess, settle down! Every time you get up, you knock my desk. He won't come any faster if you're prowling about!' Peggy said.

'The chief's secretary promised to let you know when the ship arrives,' Doris said. 'Now get on with your work. The less you get done, the more Peggy and I'll have to do.'

Eventually, Jess noticed the secretary hovering at the door. Her face was white and she seemed reluctant to enter. Jess leaped up and ran to her.

'Miss Langley,' the secretary said, 'you may want to sit down . . . I've got bad news. I . . . I'm afraid the SS Eloquence was torpedoed a short while ago . . . As far as we know, there were no survivors. I'm so sorry.'

* * *

'Please, let me go home,' Jess begged the head of department.

He sighed. He wasn't used to hysterical young women. People should have more backbone if they wanted to win the war. You'd have thought she was the only person to lose a loved one. Thousands of people had lost family members or friends and if those who'd survived didn't do their part, thousands more would be killed.

But this tiny English girl wasn't going to be much use to anyone in this state. Perhaps it was best she be sent back to Britain as quickly as they could find her a place on a ship and perhaps she'd be replaced by someone with more tenacity.

★ ★ ★

Jess hadn't had a plan. She simply knew she wanted to be back in England. The crossing had been horrendous with enormous waves and she'd spent most of the time in her cabin trying to sleep and blot out everything.

Her first thought was to go to Lestcombe Park but when she telephoned, Mrs Jenner had answered to say Gwen was in London for a few days, Phyllis was in bed with 'flu but Edna would be home shortly and what time should they expect her?

'I'll telephone again and let you know, thank you, Mrs Jenner,' she said, not able to bear the thought of spending time with tactless Edna.

What a relief it would be to go home to loving parents, but there would be no comfort at St Margaret's Vicarage.

Suddenly, she knew where she would find sympathy and support. She'd go and see Daniel's parents. Who better to share her grief? They would be devastated at the loss of their only son and they would all understand each other's pain.

* * *

Mrs Matthew's hand flew to her chest when she saw Jess on the doorstep. They didn't have a telephone, so Jess hadn't been able to warn her she was on her way.

'My goodness, Jess! How lovely to see you!' She smiled and peered around Jess

300

as if looking for someone.

She hasn't heard! Jess thought. *She doesn't know!*

'Jess? Are you all right?' Mrs Matthews asked as Jess turned white, her mouth falling open as she tried to find a way to break the news.

'I . . . I have something terrible to tell you.' The lump in Jess's throat was so large, she swallowed and tried to continue. Mrs Matthews took her arm and steered her into the kitchen where Daniel's father rose to greet her.

'Now, sit. I'll put the kettle on,' Mrs Matthews said, 'and then you can tell us all about it.'

'It's Daniel . . . ' Jess began, 'He . . . he . . . '

'I know, love.' Mrs Matthews shook her head sadly. 'He was so disappointed not to have gone with you. But you'll get another chance, I'm sure.' She patted Jess's hand and smiled.

'But he did . . . the ship . . . ' Jess couldn't finish.

Mrs Matthews frowned and shook her

head.

'No, he didn't. Or at least he hadn't gone when I spoke to him earlier this morning.' Jess stared at her. 'But the ship went down! They told me Daniel and Doc had boarded . . . '

'No!' Mrs Matthews said, her hand flying to her mouth in horror. 'Oh, you poor girl! You thought our Daniel had gone down with the ship?'

Jess nodded.

'Oh, my love! No, at the last minute Daniel and Doc Keen had to stay in Letchworth. Mr Bullock and Tony Sinclair were aboard. Sadly, they're the ones who're missing.' Mrs Matthews stood up and pulled Jess to her feet. 'Come on, love, let's go to the Post Office and we'll call Daniel.'

12

Jess checked the alarm clock by her bed. There was still an hour before she had to get up and get ready. She closed her eyes and smiled, hardly able to believe her good fortune.

Today, she would marry the most wonderful man in the world. Tom would arrive later that morning on the train with William and Gwen. Reverend and Mrs Langley had been invited but had declined.

That was William's fault. He'd taken Gwen to meet his parents and to invite them to his wedding several weeks before. He'd written to let them know he was engaged and they'd expressed their delight in him marrying Lady Gwendolyn Armstrong-Court — until the couple had visited St Margaret's Vicarage. According to Gwen, Reverend Langley's face had set in a terrible scowl and his wife had sobbed when they'd seen her.

'I thought William had told them about . . . ' Gwen said, patting her enormous stomach, 'but he hadn't. It's not as if we planned to shock them. We'd have married sooner if William could've got leave. Then no one would have had to know about the baby.'

After the visit, his parents had refused to attend the ceremony which was held, with Gwen's family's blessing, in London.

'They missed the happiest day of my life,' William said. 'I want nothing more to do with them. And once the baby's born, they'll have no part in his or her life either.'

Jess felt desperately sorry for William. He'd been in terrible danger in the Middle East and would soon return to his unit. Surely, the war and its perils had changed society's rules? Nowadays people were aware of the fragility of life. There was no time to waste on niceties and convention — people seized what happiness they could.

Jess hoped it wouldn't put her parents off coming to her wedding when they discovered William was best man, so when she invited them, she didn't mention it. She needn't have worried. They refused anyway, giving no reason. Perhaps they assumed that if their son had let them down, their daughter would too.

Always judged and found wanting, she thought, but then, they may have had a point. She placed her hands over the slight swell of her belly and smiled. Their secret — hers and Daniel's. The result of their love.

Once she'd realised he hadn't been aboard the SS Eloquence on that fateful day when it had sunk, she'd gone to him. He'd said he'd sent a letter explaining why he and Doc had remained in Letchworth and given it to Mr Bullock to deliver. On discovering the ship had gone down, he'd immediately sent a telegram but Jess was already on her way back to England, believing him dead.

He'd been waiting for her at the station

and they'd clung to each other, oblivious to the crowd of fellow passengers who parted like water flowing past a rock in the middle of a river.

'Take me home,' Jess had whispered.

With his arm wrapped around her, they'd walked through the streets and Daniel had led Jess up the stairs of his house, quietly in case his landlady hadn't gone out as she usually did in the afternoon. Once safely inside his room, Jess had clung to him, sobbing silently, hardly daring to believe he was in her arms.

He'd gently removed her spectacles and kissed the tears from her cheeks. With no care that she might be a disappointment, she wanted to make love to him. Why wait? She'd believed him lost. Now she wanted to know every part of him and would offer all of herself.

Jess undid her blouse and let it fall to the floor, throwing her head back as his lips had moved down her neck, her skin tingling with anticipation and excitement. He'd looked at her, questioningly and she'd nodded her approval as he'd gently lifted her in his arms and carried her to his bed.

And the result of that wonderful reunion now nestled deep inside her. Later that day, the excited parents of this speck of humanity would marry. Tom would give Jess away and she would marry Daniel in a small Essex church with his parents proudly watching. William would be best man, and his heavily-pregnant wife, Gwen, would be her bridesmaid, while Doc and a few others from the BTM Company as well as Phyllis and Edna would all celebrate their happiness.

Jess glanced at the clock again. It was almost time to get up. For so long, the future had been something about which she hadn't given much thought. She'd spent so much time trying to come to terms with things which had happened in the past — Clara's death, her parents' coldness, the war.

But now, with Daniel by her side and their child on the way, she wasn't afraid to look forward. One day, this dreadful war would be over and she couldn't see how the Allies could lose. Each day, their enemies' messages were being read and decisions based on that intelligence was determining the Allies' battle plans. Surely, it must result in peace one day.

When that day came, Jess knew, the work they'd done at Bletchley Park would remain secret. No one would know the hours they'd spent poring over sequences of letters — the successes and the failures. The genius and the imagination, the creativity and the resourcefulness of all involved, would never be revealed. This baby she now carried would know nothing about what its mother or father had done during the war.

But if there was any justice in this world, Jess thought, then their immense effort must surely bring the war to a close faster and with fewer lives lost than if Bletchley Park had never been. And then, this baby might be born into a world at peace. Only time would tell.

Other titles in the
Linford Romance Library:

WINGS OF A NIGHTINGALE

Alan C. Williams

It's 1941 when strong-willed Aussie nurse, Pauline Newton, arrives at Killymoor Hall, a British military hospital which has many secrets. Most crucially, it's a base for a team of Nazi saboteurs. Falling in love with the mysterious Sergeant Ray Tennyson, Pauline finds herself involved in murders, skulduggery and intrigue as they both race desperately to discover the German leaders' identity. Throughout it all, Ray and Pauline must resolve their own differences if they hope to stop the Nazis altering the War's outcome forever.

MURDER IN THE HAUNTED CASTLE

Ken Preston

Divorced Kim has come to terms with the fact that her only daughter is growing up. A last memorable holiday together before Maddie immerses herself in GCSE revision seems just the thing. But as if meeting the delectable James (no, not Bond — but close!) isn't exciting enough to throw a spanner in the works, just wait until they all get to the haunted castle. Dream holiday? More like a nightmare! But how will it end … ?

ISLAND OF MISTS

Evelyn Orange

Arasay — remote Scottish island, wildlife haven, and home to Jenna's ancestors. When she arrives to help out her great aunt in the bookshop, she's running from her past and hiding from the world. But she's not expecting to meet an attractive wildlife photographer who is also using the island to escape from previous traumas. As Jenna embraces island life and becomes closer to Jake and his family, there are secrets in the mist that could threaten their future happiness ...

ONE MAN'S LOSS

Valerie Holmes

Sir Christian Leigh-Bolton had never intended to gamble that night the vultures circled around Sir Howard. Losing heavily and in desperation, Sir Howard foolishly wagers away his inheritance, Kingsley Hall — and Christian steps in and wins the prize. Sir Howard's actions leave his sister, Eleanor, virtually homeless. Christian's honour is further tested when he makes a promise to Sir Howard, a dying man, not knowing if he can fulfil it. Meanwhile, Eleanor has taken matters into her own hands …